"I hate to take
day."

"Not a problem."

A blossoming smile made its way across her face, reminding him of the way the sun came up over the nearby hills every morning. The poetic comparison was so unlike him, he was beginning to wonder if he was coming down with something.

"You're a nice guy, Sam."

Her sweet, no-frills compliment trickled into a part of him that had been cold and dead for so long, he'd begun to think it would stay that way. He found himself smiling back at her. "You sound surprised."

"I am."

She didn't say anything more, but the lingering gaze she gave him before looking out the passenger window made his heart roll over in his chest. Normally cautious when it came to relationships, he wasn't one to go all mushy over a woman the first time he met her.

But this one had gotten to him on some level that he didn't quite understand. One thing he knew for sure, though: he didn't like it. Not one bit.

Mia Ross loves great stories. She enjoys reading about fascinating people, long-ago times and exotic places. But only for a little while, because her reality is pretty sweet. Married to her college sweetheart, she's the proud mom of two amazing kids, whose schedules keep her hopping. Busy as she is, she can't imagine trading her life for anyone else's—and she has a pretty good imagination. You can visit her online at miaross.com.

Books by Mia Ross

Love Inspired

Liberty Creek

Mending the Widow's Heart

Oaks Crossing

Her Small-Town Cowboy
Rescued by the Farmer
Hometown Holiday Reunion
Falling for the Single Mom

Barrett's Mill

Blue Ridge Reunion
Sugar Plum Season
Finding His Way Home
Loving the Country Boy

Visit the Author Profile page at Harlequin.com for more titles.

Mending the Widow's Heart

Mia Ross

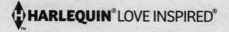

LOVE INSPIRED BOOKS

ISBN-13: 978-0-373-89960-9

Mending the Widow's Heart

www.Harlequin.com

Printed in U.S.A.

Be strong and courageous.
—*Joshua* 1:9

For all of our soldiers and their families

Acknowledgments

To Melissa Endlich and the dedicated staff at Love Inspired. These very talented folks help me make my books everything they can be.

More thanks to the gang at Seekerville (www.seekerville.net), a great place to hang out with readers—and writers.

I've been blessed with a wonderful network of supportive, encouraging family and friends. You inspire me every day!

Chapter One

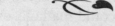

Holly Andrews was lost.

In the relatively tame wilds of New Hampshire, no less, and with a perfectly functioning navigation system. How it had happened, she had no clue, but as she swept a glance through the drizzly, empty landscape surrounding her, she couldn't come to any other conclusion.

It was early June, and the trip from Boston north to Portsmouth had been easy enough. From there, the drive had gone so well, on wide highways bordered by enormous trees and mile after mile of wildflowers. For the past hour, though, she'd been hugging her side of a narrow two-lane road that could barely be classified as paved. So far, she'd narrowly avoided four humongous tractors, three runaway cows and a flock of white geese that had taken their sweet time crossing to a pond on the other side.

"Mom?"

Forcing sweetness into her voice to cover her irritation, she smiled into the rearview mirror at her eight-year-old son. "Yes, Chase?"

"Are we lost?"

"Of course not," she insisted in the most upbeat voice she could manage. As a former military wife, she'd had plenty of practice with that. Tapping the navigation screen, she added, "The computer knows right where we are."

"But do you?"

Sometimes she thought he was way too smart for his own good. *Like his father*, she added sadly. It had been two years since she'd buried him in a hero's grave to honor his devotion to the country he'd loved. But every once in a while, when she least expected it, the darkness that had dominated the end of Brady's life still reached out and ambushed her.

Calling up every ounce of determination she had, she pushed the grimness aside and focused on getting them to her aunt's new home in the quaintly named village of Liberty Creek. After fighting the past for so long, Holly believed it would be refreshing to put that behind her and look to the future. With their savings nearly gone, her part-time retail work wouldn't be enough to support them, and she recognized that a new career for her was an absolute must. The trouble was that while she'd been caring full-time for her family, she'd sunk to the bottom of her own priority list. Somewhere along the line she'd lost sight of the things she'd once enjoyed so much.

Time away from Boston was exactly what she needed to help her focus on what should come next. If she couldn't figure out a way to be content there, she'd have no choice but to uproot them and start over somewhere else. She hated to take Chase from the only home he'd known, but she knew it would be better to move him soon so he could make new friends more easily than he would in high school.

But right now, she needed to find this seemingly invisible town. She was just about to pull over and put out an SOS when she noticed a crisp white sign up ahead.

Welcome to Liberty Creek.

She followed the gentle curve, craning her neck to make sure no surprises popped up out of the mist. At least now she could be sure she was in the right place. Her thought was promptly confirmed by the system chirping, "You have reached your destination."

"Yeah, thanks for nothing," Holly muttered, reaching over to mute the annoying computer voice. Now that the car was silent, she could make out the smack of large raindrops as they began pelting the windshield. When she switched on the wipers she'd forgotten to replace before leaving, they left unhelpful streaks across the bug-spattered glass. Perfect. For Chase's sake, she summoned a chipper tone. "Almost there."

"Good job, Mom. I knew you could do it."

Her ray of sunshine, she mused with a smile. Ever since the moment when the delivery room nurse settled him in Holly's arms, Chase had been the single bright spot in more of her days than she cared to recall. She honestly had no idea where she'd be without him.

"I forgot to mention that I got an email from your teacher this morning. You aced the assessment they had you take to let you leave school a couple weeks early."

"That's cool," he said in a matter-of-fact tone that told her he'd expected the result. "The tests were easy, and Mrs. Graves said I finished in record time."

"So we should be looking at colleges, then?" Though she was teasing, she was immensely proud of Chase's accomplishments, both in and out of the classroom. Considering all they'd been through as a family, it was a blessing to know that her boy had managed to keep his head on straight.

"Maybe next year. I'm hoping to get Miss Farmer for third grade."

His comment gave her a twinge of guilt for her earlier thoughts about moving, but she shoved the negative emotion aside. "Why is that?"

"She likes the Red Sox," he said, as if it should have been obvious.

But Holly knew him better than that, and she couldn't help smiling. "What else?"

"Well..." He stalled, then laughed. "She's pretty, and she adopted a dog from a shelter and named him Fenway."

That sounded more like it, Holly thought as she navigated yet another turn. The weak afternoon light did little to cut through the descending fog, and she had to really concentrate to keep her car on the proper side of the unmarked road. Because she was focusing so intently on that, her next glance into the distance made her squeak with surprise and hit the brakes.

There, not twenty feet away, stood a one-lane covered bridge. Sporting faded white paint and a walkway along one side, it conjured up all the Currier and Ives Christmas cards she'd gotten over the years. As she drove across the wooden planking and out the other end, the mist parted around a scene straight out of an artist's dream: a village that looked like it had been built centuries ago and had somehow managed to stay there.

Buildings made of brick and classic New England clapboards lined Main Street, their green-and-white-striped awnings dripping water onto people scurrying to get out of the rain. The street was paved, but well-worn cobblestones ran along both sides in a charming nod to the past. In the square, a white gazebo was nestled under massive trees that looked old enough to predate the town, if that was even possible. The business district covered less than three blocks, so it took her about two seconds to find the place she was looking for: Ellie's Bakery and Bike Rentals.

After parking in an open spot across the street, she swiveled to look back at Chase. "It's pouring, and I should only be a sec. Do you want to wait here where it's dry?"

"I kind of have to use the bathroom."

Grinning, she tilted her head. "Kind of?" He nodded, and she said, "Let's go, then."

As he unbuckled his seat belt, she caught herself remembering all the years of dealing with car seats and toddler boosters. Had it really been just a year ago that he'd outgrown the last of them? Mom was right—your own childhood dragged by, but when you were a mom, your kids grew up at warp speed.

Since the rain seemed to have settled in for the duration, Holly pulled up the hood on Chase's sweatshirt, and they made a run for the antique front door. From what she could see through the glass, the place looked deserted. There was no Closed sign posted, so she yanked on the brass handle and was relieved when the door opened. She could hear muted big band music playing in the kitchen, but out front the scattered tables and long lunch counter stood completely empty.

"Hello?" She waited for a moment, then called out again.

She was just about to give up when something ominous rumbled underneath a set of old-fashioned ice-cream soda dispensers. It sounded like a displeased grizzly bear, and she instinctively drew Chase back a step when a pair of enormous hands appeared on the countertop. They were connected to a set of muscular forearms clad in denim, and as their owner appeared, it was all she could do to keep from turning and bolting back the way they'd come.

Six and a half feet, easy, he brought to mind

the massive trees in the square. Tall, unyielding, built to withstand a storm and keep on going. His light brown hair was a little too long for her taste, and his icy blue eyes held a laser sharpness that would make anyone think twice about approaching him. "Can I help you?"

His less-than-friendly demeanor was off-putting, but she forced herself to smile. "I'm so sorry to intrude like this, but I'm Holly Andrews. Daphne Mills's niece," she added, hoping that dropping her famous aunt's name would gain her some points. It didn't seem to work, but he didn't ask her to leave, so she boldly forged ahead. "When she hurt her back, she asked us to come help out until she feels better. We drove up from Boston today, and she said she was going to leave an envelope for me here."

The man's eyes darkened to a stony gray, and Holly replayed her introduction in her head, wondering what she might have said to warrant such a cool reaction. But the gloomy look vanished as quickly as it had appeared, and she chalked her impression up to a long drive and the cloudy weather.

"Daphne mentioned something about that to me the other day," he finally answered. "I think Gran put it behind here somewhere."

As he began to disappear under the counter again, she moved forward to get his attention. "I hate to bother you, but my son needs to use the restroom. Could you point it out for us?"

He obliged her, and Chase zoomed off in the direction the man had nodded. That left Holly more or less alone with a stranger, and since he was obviously a friend of her favorite aunt, she decided that just wouldn't do. "I'm sorry, but I didn't catch your name."

He muttered something beneath his breath and rose with a grimace. "Yeah, I still forget sometimes. Sam Calhoun. I'd shake your hand, but—" Frowning, he showed her his filthy palms.

The collection of grim expressions he'd displayed, combined with his comment about sometimes forgetting to introduce himself, intrigued her more than they should have. Something about him screamed "wounded," but she couldn't quite figure out why. Then she noticed the outline of something rectangular dangling under his T-shirt, and she had her answer. "Military, right?"

"I was an Army Ranger." His eyes narrowed into cynical slits. "How'd you know?"

"Just a hunch." She nearly left it at that, then recalled her therapist's advice about not hiding her difficult past and took a quiet breath before explaining. "My late husband, Brady, was a Marine."

The chill in Sam's eyes warmed a bit, and he gave her a look filled with the sympathy of someone all too familiar with her circumstances. Fortunately, Chase trotted in to rejoin them, saving her the awkwardness of either explaining further or pretending that there was nothing more to tell.

More than once, she'd caught herself wondering how things would be for her now if she'd never met Brady in the first place. But then she wouldn't have Chase, and her life was infinitely better for being his mom. So, despite the fact that Brady had caused her more heartache than she'd once thought humanly possible, she did her best to feel grateful for the good things he'd left behind.

"Chase, this is Sam Calhoun, a friend of Aunt Daphne's. Sam, this is my son, Chase."

Her son stared up at the towering man but bravely held his hand out over the counter. "It's nice to meet you, sir."

A hint of a smile lifted the corner of Sam's mouth as they shook. "Same here."

Chase's blue eyes drifted away, lighting on a glass display case filled with several varieties of cookies. "Are those fresh?"

"Kids like to stop in on their way home

from school, so my grandmother makes sure there's snacks for them to enjoy. She brought 'em outta the kitchen about an hour ago. Is that fresh enough for you?"

Chase nodded, and Sam motioned them to two stools. After washing his hands, he got them each a plate and set a delicious-smelling assortment in front of them. "Help yourselves, on the house." When Holly opened her mouth to object, he cut her off. "You're both soaked from the rain. It's the least I can do."

Deciding it would be rude to refuse his kind gesture, she chose one covered in chocolate icing and sprinkles. When she bit into it, it fell apart in her mouth as she hummed in appreciation. "Amazing. Now that I've heard it again, Calhoun sounds familiar. Is that the name I saw on the brass sign next to the bridge?"

Pride softened Sam's angular features, and he nodded. "In 1820, Jeremiah Calhoun and his two brothers crossed the creek with nothing to their names but three teams of oxen and their wagons. They were top-notch blacksmiths, but there was no ironworks around here at the time. They opened Liberty Creek Forge to supply metal for themselves and other businesses that had started springing up. They built the bridge a couple years later so folks could get here easier. Some of them liked the area well enough to stick around."

"And the rest is history," she said, smiling at the appealing homespun story.

Having been raised in Savannah, she had a reverence for the past that had followed her throughout her life. She'd hoped to use that to create some kind of connection with this enigmatic man, but her efforts failed miserably. For some reason, the tentative light in his eyes dimmed, leaving them a flat grayish-blue that made her think of the storm clouds still hovering outside the windows.

Looking away, he pulled a pint carton of milk out of a cooler for Chase, then took two sturdy-looking mugs from a set of open shelves that ran the length of the wall opposite where they were sitting. "There's a new pot of coffee. Would you like some?"

"Please." One sip nearly put her on the floor, but she managed to swallow the jolt of caffeine without gagging. She reached out for a bowl of nondairy creamer and emptied a few of the thimble-sized portions into her mug.

"Too strong?"

Apparently, Sam was more observant than most, and she smiled to ease any insult she might have caused. "A little. I'm not used to coffee that'll hold a spoon upright."

"Sorry."

It occurred to her that when he'd been relaying the story of his family's legacy, Sam had seemed comfortable enough talking to her. But now that they were speaking more spontaneously, his conversational style was decidedly sparser. It reminded her of an actor who was adept at delivering his lines but stumbled while fielding questions during an interview.

She'd seen that kind of behavior many times at the veterans' hospital, and she suspected that Sam was still waging a battle against something that had followed him home from wherever he'd been stationed. While Holly felt compassion for the former soldier, warning bells were clanging in her head so loudly, she wouldn't be surprised to learn that Sam could hear them, too.

Still struggling to leave those horrific memories behind, she was committed to starting a new life with her son as far from the military as she could get. She was rapidly approaching thirty, and now that she'd made it through the worst storm she could imagine, it was time to make some serious plans for the future. For both her and Chase.

They'd spend their summer with Aunt Daphne, getting her back on her feet and enjoying this picturesque part of New Hampshire to the hilt. Then, in August, Holly would be ready to make some solid decisions about their futures and get Chase registered in a new school if they found themselves somewhere other than Boston. Nowhere in those plans did she have the time or the energy to take on another emotionally scarred soldier who may or may not become whole again. Chase was only six when Brady died, so he had hazy images of his father. To her mind, his ignorance was a blessing considering the tragic way Brady's life had ended.

But now her son was old enough to get attached to people and be devastated if they were suddenly yanked out of his life. For her sake and Chase's, Holly knew that the smartest thing she could do was keep Sam Calhoun at a nice, safe distance.

Sam had never been the chatty type.

His mother had often accused him of being a poster child for the staid New Englander who didn't have much to say but meant every word that came out of his mouth. Still, in thirty years of living he'd never found himself tongue-tied around a woman. Until now.

Holly Andrews was more than easy on the eyes. A few blond strands had escaped her ponytail, framing her brilliant blue eyes in a halo of curls. When she'd pegged him as former military, he'd braced himself for the awkward moment when he'd have to explain where he'd served and why he was back.

To his great relief, she didn't ask. Probably because she was familiar with veterans and could sense that he didn't want to talk about his experience. The interesting thing was, she didn't treat him like someone who needed to be handled with kid gloves the way so many folks did. Instead, she'd given him sympathy and understanding. For someone who'd dealt with every conceivable reaction during the past year, Sam found her matter-of-fact approach to him a refreshing change.

Realizing that her drink was nearly gone, he asked, "Would you like a refill on that?"

"That'd be great. It was a long trip, and we still have to drive to Auntie D's and unpack."

"Auntie D?" he echoed in disbelief as he poured coffee into her mug and added some hot water to make it more to her taste. "That's what you call Daphne Mills, the greatest actress of her generation?"

"Oh, that's just a bunch of hype invented by her agent." Holly waved it off with a laugh. "She'd be the first to tell you there were actresses better than her. Not many, of course, but a few," she added with a fond smile.

"I guess she'd know." Then he remembered what had brought Holly into the bakery in the first place. "I think that envelope you were asking about is back here somewhere. Gimme a sec."

"Don't rush. If we're not in the way, I'd rather hang out here until it quits raining, anyway."

"According to the weatherman, this storm's not moving off till tomorrow morning."

"Oh, well." Glancing at her son, she shrugged a delicate shoulder. "Them's the breaks, right, bud?"

"We won't melt," he assured her brightly.

She rewarded his optimism with a proud mother's smile and slit open the envelope Sam had given her. A pile of cash spilled onto the counter, followed by a house key.

She let out a sound that was half moan and half laugh. "Oh, Auntie, what're you thinking?"

"Whoa," Chase commented. "That's a lotta money."

"It certainly is," Holly replied, shaking her head as if she couldn't quite believe it herself.

Sam was trying hard not to snoop, but it was impossible to miss the large, scrawling message on the pale pink stationery.

Get whatever you want, Peaches.

Reaching back inside, Holly pulled another piece of paper from the envelope. She opened the note and studied it with a frown. When she started spinning the page, he felt compelled to ask, "Something wrong?"

"I'm assuming this is meant to be a map."

When she turned it for him to see, he realized that even a local like him would have trouble following the vague drawing anywhere. "City folks like your aunt aren't much for giving directions. They like their GPS."

"It's very helpful," Holly informed him primly. "I managed to get all the way here from Boston using it."

"To the town, sure, but you won't find Daphne's place that way. That road's not even on a state map."

He seldom engaged anyone so directly, especially not someone he'd just met. Why had he chosen this afternoon—and this particular woman—to change his approach? No explanation immediately came to mind, but he couldn't help feeling that something important had just happened to him. Something bigger than an out-of-towner needing directions.

It gave him a sliver of hope that he might be able to regain his emotional footing, after all. Since his return, he'd felt like a stranger in the hometown that had always been a haven from the world. No matter what he'd tried, that impression had stubbornly remained, leaving him convinced that as much as he loved the town that his family had built from nothing, it might not be the best place for him anymore.

What would it be like to start over? he'd wondered more than once. To go someplace where no one knew him and wouldn't ask about things he'd prefer never to talk about again? Sometimes, after a particularly difficult day, moving away was the only choice that made any sense to him.

When it dawned on him that Holly was speaking to him, he yanked his wandering mind back to their conversation.

"She told us that's one of the things she likes most about Liberty Creek," Holly went on. "After dodging Hollywood paparazzi for so long, she's thrilled about having her privacy back and being treated like a regular person."

Sam chuckled. "No offense, but there's nothing regular about her. She's one of a kind."

When Holly tilted her head and gazed up at him, he wondered if he'd stepped over some unseen line of etiquette. He'd just met her, after all, and she could easily misinterpret what he'd intended to be a compliment. He'd never had much luck reading women, so he waited anxiously for her to say something.

"I think so, too," she finally agreed, adding a cute grin. "Just don't tell her I said so. She'll never let me hear the end of it."

It didn't occur to him that he'd been holding his breath until it came out in a rush. Hoping to mask his bizarre reaction to her, he held out his hand. "Deal."

As they shook, Holly's hand felt small and vulnerable in his, but her grip was firm. *Trusting* was the word that leapt into his mind, and he sternly pushed it aside. Nice as she seemed, there was no way he'd drag a woman into his wreck of a life, especially one with such a young child. Even though every word she said in that lilting Southern accent of hers made him want to smile.

He'd just made that decision when she said, "I hate to impose, but is there any way you could help me get out there? She's coming home from the hospital on Friday, and I have a lot to do before then, so I'd like to get started first thing in the morning. Even a new map would be better than this," she added, waving the useless drawing before tossing it on the counter.

"Sure." Sam reached for an order pad and pen, then stopped. His parents had drummed hospitality into their children's heads since they were old enough to grasp the concept. It certainly didn't include sketching roads on a piece of paper for a visitor who'd probably get lost once she left Main Street. "Actually, I'm doing the rehab work out at her place, and the new fixtures for the kitchen and bathroom came in today. I was planning to take them out there later, but if you give me a minute, we can go now. That way, you can follow me and learn the way."

"Oh, that's not necessary." Reaching out, she rested a hand on her son's shoulder in a motherly gesture. "I'm sure we can find it, and I hate to interrupt what you're doing."

"You've had a long day already," Sam argued, unsure of why he was fighting with her about this. Most of the time, he let people make their own choices and didn't worry too much about the outcome. For some reason, this was different, and he tried again. "It's still raining, and you've probably got a few suitcases. If I give you a hand, the unloading will go faster."

"I can't argue with that." Letting out a tired sigh, she smiled at Chase. "Right now, I'd give anything for a warm bath and some dry clothes."

"Me, too," the boy chimed in eagerly.

That was the closest he'd come to complaining, and Sam had to admit that he was impressed with the kid's upbeat attitude. *Probably got it from his mother,* Sam mused before shoving the thought away. "Okay, then it's settled. I'll be right back."

"I'll be here."

She gave him a grateful smile before focusing on the rest of Daphne's letter. It was a good thing, too, because the exchange of those few simple words had unleashed a torrent of emotions in Sam. As vivid as the day they'd first appeared, they made his chest twist with a pain so strong, he wondered for the countless time if he'd be dragging it around with him like some invisible anchor until the undertaker finally put him in the ground.

Running his hand over the dog tags he wore beneath his shirt, he closed his eyes and waited for the worst of it to pass. As usual, the intensity eased, but the remorse he still felt left a bitter taste in his mouth. Someday, he might be able to hear someone say, "I'll be here," and not flash back to the darkest, most horrific day of his life.

But not today.

Chapter Two

Holly was fairly certain that if Sam had left her to her own devices, she'd have driven right past the road that led to the long, winding driveway of her aunt's new home. One unmarked side street led to another and another, which fed into an isolated dead end that held exactly three houses. She got the feeling that her guide was finding his way through the outskirts of Liberty Creek using an inherited sense of where things in his hometown had been standing since the founders had first hacked it out of the forest.

She'd never been much for school, but being a history buff, that class had always held a special appeal for her. She recalled that New Hampshire was one of the original thirteen colonies and had played a pivotal role in the Americans' fight for independence. If those long-ago Calhoun brothers were any indication of the local residents' spirit, she had no trouble believing that men like them—strong and stubborn—had played a key role in the patriots' eventual victory.

Sam's pickup finally signaled a turn onto a rutted lane that looked more like a deer path than a driveway. When she got her first look at the house, she groaned out loud. "Oh, Auntie. Have you lost your mind?"

Chase leaned in to get a clearer view between the front headrests. "Didn't Sam say he was fixing the house?"

"Yes."

"It looks like he should tear it down instead."

She couldn't have summed up the property's condition any better, but she was wary of agreeing for fear that he'd repeat her comments and hurt their sensitive relative's feelings. The sprawling farmhouse must have stood on many more acres years ago, and the trees growing around it were the same vintage as the ones she'd admired in the town square. The porch that stretched across the front of the house wasn't quite done, and the front steps were nowhere to be seen. Entire sections of boards had been replaced, but most of the antiquated windows remained. The end wall was painted a mellow cream, and a pair of wine-colored shutters leaning against it gave her a glimpse of Sam's plans for the exterior. She could envision it looking classic and stunning when it was finished, but for now, the kindest description she could invent was "work in progress."

Sam parked near the front porch and climbed out of his truck. Avoiding the puddles, he strolled toward Holly's car while she sat there trying to come up with something encouraging to say about the dilapidated farmhouse her aunt had bought on a whim for her retirement home.

When she stepped out, she blurted out the only positive remark she could think of. "It's in a real pretty spot."

Cocking an eyebrow in obvious amusement, he said, "I know the house isn't much to look at now, but it's actually better than it was when I started in the spring."

"Was it falling down the hill?"

"Not a chance. This place was built of solid oak, and it'll outlast all of us. It was empty for a while, but with a little work, it'll be amazing."

She stared up at him waiting for the punch line, but judging by his earnest expression, he wasn't yanking her chain. He sounded confident, not in the cocky way some guys could, but in the solid, dependable way a girl would be able to count on.

So, since she wasn't exactly Miss DIY, Holly decided that she didn't have a choice other than to trust his assessment. "If you say so."

"I do."

The clouds in his eyes lightened, and the corner of his mouth crinkled in a half-hearted motion that made her wonder what it would take to coax an actual smile from him. Not that it was up to her, of course. She was just curious.

"So," he went on, "I'm guessing you've got a trunk full of suitcases."

"We have a few things," she retorted, irritated by the thinly veiled display of chauvinism. She'd gotten enough of that from other men to last her for the rest of her life. Overwhelmed by Brady's deteriorating condition, she'd made the mistake of allowing other people to do things for her that she could have handled herself. It had led them to view her as helpless and, after a while, she'd been alarmed to find she'd started agreeing with them. One of the many things she was determined to change as she took charge of her life again. "It was nice of you to offer your help, but we'll be fine. Chase can manage the smaller bags and I can get the big ones."

"No, you can't."

Sam's condescending tone got her back up, and she glared at him. "Excuse me?"

"Easy now," he soothed with a hand in the air. "I just meant a lady shouldn't be carrying her own luggage when there's a guy around who's willing to do it for her."

She refused to take that bait and stood with her arms crossed, scowling up at him for all she was worth. After a few seconds of that, he shoved his hands in the back pockets of his well-worn jeans and sighed. "How 'bout we do it together? Those clouds aren't going anywhere, and I'd hate to see all your stuff get drenched."

Holly glanced into the distance to see that he was right about the rain and decided there was absolutely no point in being obstinate. This time, anyway. "Okay, that makes sense."

Reaching back into the car, she popped the trunk as he muttered something under his breath. It wasn't flattering, but he was taking time out of his day to help her so she opted to let it go. He reminded her of a displeased grizzly bear most of the time, and she wasn't keen on pushing him too far and alienating him altogether. As the contractor on this large job, he'd be around a lot, and she figured it would go better if they could at least be civil to one another.

Eyeing their pile of luggage, he shook his head but didn't comment on her heavy traveling style. Instead, he plucked out two enormous cases crammed to the gills and carried them to the finished half of the porch without complaint. Whoa, she thought with honest admiration as she picked up two of the smaller bags. He was even stronger than he looked.

They quickly emptied the trunk and then paused while Holly fished out the key Aunt Daphne had left at the bakery for her. As she turned the knob, Sam stopped her with a hand on her arm.

"Did Daphne warn you about Pandora?"

That sounded ominous, and Holly couldn't help giggling. "You mean, as in 'Don't open that box'?"

She delivered the last few words in a horror movie narrator voice, and to her utter surprise, he laughed. She'd barely been able to get a smirk out of him until now, so the bright sound astonished her. Quite honestly, she wasn't sure he had that kind of humor in him, and it was nice to discover that he did.

"No, I mean, the big black cat named Pandora. I never got the connection till now, but she can be a troublemaker, so her name definitely fits." Looking down at Chase, he went on, "She's the queen around here, and you'll do well to remember that."

Holly wasn't much of a cat person, so his advice seemed slightly over the top. "You're kidding, right?"

"Nope."

He looked deadly serious, but she simply couldn't picture herself kowtowing to any ball of fur smaller than her. "Fine. Can we go in now?"

In answer, he swung the door open and stepped back to let her go ahead of him. Before she had a chance to set even one foot inside, a streak of black tore through the hallway and disappeared under the plastic that was stretched across the wide staircase that led to the second floor.

Feeling a little off-kilter in the middle of a strange house in a town she'd never visited, Holly forgot Sam was even there until he cleared his throat.

"Hmm?" she asked.

"I could use a hand with the door."

Idiot, Holly scolded herself, reaching past him to push open what was obviously a freshly repaired screen door. "Sorry. The cat spooked me, and I spaced out there for a second. I guess these should go upstairs."

"The two guest rooms are in the front of the house. They have the nicest views, so Daphne had me finish those first."

"Cool!" Chase approved, ducking under the barrier in much the same way Pandora had. As he pounded up the raw wooden steps, Holly took a moment to get a better sense of the place that Sam had such high hopes for.

The entry must have been a grand foyer back in the day, but the cosmetic issues outside were nothing compared to the demolition that had gutted the interior. From walls to ceilings, everything had been stripped back to the studs and was in the process of being rebuilt. The wide oak planks on the floor had been sanded down to their natural state, and there were patches of various stains around the living room, as if someone was testing them for color.

"I know it's a mess right now," he said, giving voice to her less-than-optimistic thought, "but I'll have it done in time."

"In time for what?"

Glancing upstairs, he went on in a muted voice. "Don't tell anyone else 'cause it's supposed to be a surprise, but Daphne wants to fly your whole family up here in November to celebrate Thanksgiving with her. That was before we knew how bad the termites had gotten to the timbers over the years, but she's still set on making it happen. It's my job to make sure you all have a nice place to stay while you're here."

"That sounds like something she'd do," Holly commented fondly. "During her acting career, she lived in big houses and adored having company. I guess now she'll just invite everyone here instead."

"I'd imagine so. Could you pull that plastic back for me?"

Holly peeled away one side of it for Sam to go through and followed him up. At the top of the stairs, he turned down a short hallway and stopped between two massive doors that looked like they were made of mahogany. One was open, and she saw Chase inside, testing the bounciness of the mattress on his bed. She nearly scolded him, then thought better of it. He'd been so great all day, a little trampoline time seemed like a good reward. At least he'd taken his shoes off before climbing on it, she noted proudly.

Leaving him to his fun, she opened the other bedroom door for Sam, and what she saw inside made her smile. Daphne had always kept a special guest room for Holly to use during visits to Beverly Hills, and she'd duplicated it in her new house. The walls were painted a cloudy blue, and white trim around the windows framed lush green scenery that promised to be beautiful when the sun finally came out. From the four-poster bed to the chair in front of the small desk, it was all here, and Holly immediately felt like she belonged.

Strolling in behind her, Sam set her bags inside the walk-in closet. "From the way you're smiling, I take it I got everything right."

"Perfect. It feels like home."

"That's what she was after, so I'm glad you approve. Have a look around while I get the rest of your stuff."

While he was gone, she went to the other window to see if her room looked out on more than the quiet landscape. She pulled aside a lacy curtain and discovered that she had a distant peekaboo view of the historic bridge. Now that she was finally here, she couldn't shake the feeling that the centuries-old structure had guided her toward a better place than the one she'd recently left. Wondering what lay ahead for Chase and her, she stared out at it until she heard Sam's boots coming up the stairs again.

The time for daydreaming was over. Aunt

Daphne was coming home soon, and Holly had a lot of work to do before then.

Turning away from the foggy view, Holly asked, "So, is there a tour?"

"Sure."

Since he didn't know what else to say, Sam motioned her out the door. Fortunately for him, she was the bubbly, curious type, which meant he didn't have to do much more than answer her questions. While he took her through the house, she pressed him for all sorts of details about the rehab that was under way. The roof, the porches, the architectural touches—she was interested in it all, and Sam was only too happy to keep her talking. That accent of hers was downright hypnotizing.

In the kitchen, she turned to him with amazement lighting those incredible eyes. "I can't believe you're doing this all by yourself."

"Actually, a couple friends come and help out when I need extra hands." Sensing that it was time to come clean, he paused to clear his throat. "I think you should know Daphne hurt her back when she tripped on something that got left on the main stairway. It was an accident, but I feel awful about it. We all do."

That it had been a part-timer who'd carelessly left his toolbox where it didn't belong didn't matter to Sam. That he'd fired the guy on the spot was beside the point. Sam was in charge of this project, and to him that meant he was responsible for Daphne's injury. He wasn't crazy about having to apologize for other people's mistakes, but he wouldn't shirk the blame, either. Someday it might not be necessary for him to work within such a tight budget, and he'd be able to hire a skilled full-time crew. But right now he didn't have a choice. Running a small business was tough in the best of times, and with the local economy still reeling from all kinds of setbacks, he couldn't afford to pay the rates professional subcontractors charged.

He held his breath, waiting to see how she'd react to the news, but Holly gave him a reassuring look. "She told me all about it. She doesn't blame you even the tiniest bit, and neither do I. Things like that happen, and she's going to be fine."

"Thanks for saying that. I appreciate it." Now that he'd fessed up, Sam felt as if a huge weight had been lifted from his shoulders, and he relaxed enough to be friendlier. "Come on, and I'll show you the room we set up for Daphne to use while she's on the mend. It has a full bath next to it, so I think it'll work well for her. I just finished painting the trim yesterday, so it might still be tacky in spots."

The large back parlor had a wide bank of windows, and he'd already moved Daphne's bedroom furniture down from the master bedroom. A huge TV was mounted over the fireplace, in clear view of the bed set up on the opposite wall. Trailing a hand over the hand-carved rosewood mantel, Holly peered out the windows that overlooked the backyard. "Wow, it's even worse than the front. I think I saw Tarzan up in one of those trees."

"That's why she got such a good deal on this place. Well, that and the termites."

Holly typed something on her phone and backtracked into the kitchen. Sam watched her throw open one cupboard after another, then both sides of the shiny new French door–style fridge. When she glanced up, she asked, "Why are there two bowls up there?"

"Pandora likes to eat there. That way, she can keep an eye on everything."

"Seriously?" He nodded, and she laughed. "This is one spoiled cat, but I guess I better go along with it, since that's what she's used to."

When she finally reached the last cupboard, the amused look on her face told him that she'd found what she was hunting for on a bare shelf. Taking out another of Daphne's personalized envelopes, she read the note out loud. "Get whatever you think we should have, Peaches."

Holly opened it, and inside were more hundred-dollar bills than Sam had ever seen in one place. "She left you money already."

"That was for Chase and me, in case we need something. This—" she held up an impressive fan of Benjamins "—is for food. Totally different."

"Okay," he replied, still unable to believe how much cash Daphne kept on hand. "While I'm thinking of it, you gotta tell me why she calls you Peaches."

Holly laughed. "It's an old nickname. When I was little, I wouldn't eat anything other than peaches. If Mom wanted me to try something new, she had to mix some of them in or I wouldn't touch it. Dad started calling me Peaches, and it stuck."

Looking at the nearly empty shelves, he said, "Looks like you've got some shopping to do. Daphne mostly eats out, either on her own or with friends. She told me she can hardly work the microwave, but I figured she was kidding."

"No, she was totally serious. She's a people person, and machines confound her. But we can't take her to a restaurant for every meal in her condition, so when we spoke on the phone last week, I warned her that we'd need some groceries."

"I can help with that, if you want," he blurted without thinking. Despite his earlier wariness, something about this spunky single mom made him want to step up and give her a hand. It wasn't a date or anything, he assured himself, and he could catch up on his lengthy to-do list tomorrow. The work wasn't going anywhere. "I'll put away those supplies I brought and meet you out at my truck."

She didn't say anything to that, and he wondered what he might have said wrong. Then it hit him that she might not be inclined to get into a stranger's car with her son, and he amended his offer. "You can follow me out there if you'd rather do it that way."

Gazing up at him, she studied him for several long, uncomfortable moments. Then, to his great relief, she smiled. "Auntie D trusts you. That's good enough for me."

Sam felt as if he'd just scored a touchdown, but the swift connection he'd made with this engaging woman was unsettling, so he kept it to himself. After shuttling in the new kitchen faucet and fixtures for Daphne's bathroom, he went back to his truck. Reaching behind the seat, he grabbed a clean shirt to replace the grimy one he was wearing. The bottle of water he found underneath it wasn't cold, but it felt good going down, and he finished it off while he waited.

A few minutes later, Holly and Chase joined him, and he opened the passenger door for them. The boy eagerly jumped in, but Holly hung back, rewarding Sam with another of her heartwarming smiles before climbing inside. He'd counted four different versions of that expression, and he wondered how many more she had tucked away, ready to be pulled out for the right occasion. He'd just met her, and she was already drawing him in like some kind of feminine magnet.

He really needed to get a grip, he thought as he settled into the driver's seat. Out of necessity, he'd pulled into himself after leaving the service, unwilling to subject anyone to the turmoil of emotions that seemed to have taken up permanent residence inside him. His little sister had accused him of becoming a hermit, and while he believed her assessment was on the melodramatic side, he couldn't deny that it wasn't too far off the truth.

One day, he'd be almost like his old self: confident, capable and ready to take on whatever life threw at him. And the next, he'd take an enormous step back into the mire that had dominated his perception of the world since his injuries had sent him home. The physical wounds had long since healed, but inside the scars sometimes felt as fresh as if they'd happened yesterday. He'd give anything to go back and relive that day, find some way to make it end differently.

But he couldn't. He regretted that more than he'd ever be able to convey, and there was absolutely nothing he could do about it.

Squaring his shoulders with determination, Sam put aside the past and focused on the misty view outside the windshield. Unfortunately, in the enclosed cab, he caught a whiff of Holly's perfume. With a mental groan, he identified the flowery scent: roses. He'd always had a fondness for roses.

"There's a small market in town," he explained as he headed for the highway. "But considering the fact that Daphne's cupboards are pretty much empty, I'm thinking you need something more than a few cans of soup and a loaf of bread. Waterford has a big new grocery store that should do the trick."

"Oh, it's not far, is it? It's getting late, and I hate to take up the rest of your day."

"Not a problem."

A blossoming smile made its way across her face, reminding him of the way the sun came up over the nearby hills every morning. The poetic comparison was so unlike him, he was beginning to wonder if he was coming down with something.

"You're a nice guy, Sam."

Her sweet, no-frills compliment trickled into a part of him that had been cold and dead for so long, he'd begun to think it would stay that way. His brain was clanging a warning, but the rest of him apparently wasn't listening because he found himself smiling back at her. "You sound surprised."

"I am."

She didn't say anything more, but the lingering gaze she gave him before looking out the passenger window made his heart roll over in his chest. Normally cautious when it came to relationships, he wasn't one to go all mushy over a woman the first time he met her.

But this one had gotten to him on some level that he didn't quite understand. One thing he knew for sure, though: he didn't like it. Not one bit.

Chapter Three

The next morning, Sam was clearing equipment from the bed of his work truck when he heard the kitchen screen door of Daphne's house quietly creak open. He knew the sound of someone sneaking out, and he peered over the unruly boxwood hedge that separated his yard from hers. "Morning."

Chase's head snapped around, a guilty look on his face. "Hi."

There was something about this kid that really appealed to him, so Sam decided to play it cool. "Headed to work?"

The boy grinned and shook his head. "Just checking things out. Mom said it was too muddy yesterday."

"Sounds like a mom." Sam wasn't used to dealing with children, and he hunted for something else to say. "Wanna give me a hand?"

"I can't leave Auntie D's yard."

It was a good rule, and Sam didn't want him getting into trouble. Then inspiration hit, and he asked, "Have you got a baseball glove?"

"In the car. Why?"

"I'm ready for a break. We could play catch over the hedge if you want."

"Cool! I'll be right back."

Skirting around the side porch, he scrambled up the driveway to where Holly's car was parked. Sam expected to hear the slamming of a car door, but Chase made barely a sound opening and closing it before running back. *Smart kid*, Sam thought with a grin as he went into the garage to find his own glove and a baseball. They were under a pile of junk on his work bench, covered in dust. And one of the strings on his glove was considerably shorter than the others, with telltale gnaw marks that alerted him he had a mouse.

More like mice, he amended with a grimace. In his experience, the little pests always came with friends and were hard to get rid of. Just as he felt his chipper mood starting its usual nosedive, something incredible happened.

It stopped. As if someone had reached out to catch a ball on its way to the ground, his demeanor reversed course all on its own and began lifting again. Sam had never experienced anything even remotely like this, and he had no idea what to make of it. Since Chase was anxiously bouncing from one sneaker to the other on his side of the hedge, Sam put aside his bewilderment, banged the dirt and sawdust from his glove and tossed his throwing partner an easy pop fly.

After a few of those back and forth, Chase finally complained. "Come on, Sam. I'm not a baby."

He laughed and put some more muscle into the next one. "Better?"

"Yeah, thanks."

"No problem. Y'know, you're pretty good at this. Who taught you to throw?"

"Mom did. She's got a good arm for a girl."

"Does she like baseball, too?" Sam didn't know what made him ask that, but now that he had, it dawned on him that his curiosity about his new neighbor hadn't gone away overnight the way he'd expected it to.

"Kinda," the boy replied as if it baffled him. "She grew up rooting for Atlanta, but she met my dad at a Boston doubleheader, so now she likes the Red Sox."

It was the first Sam had heard either of them talk about the boy's father, and it made him wonder about the details of his death.

He'd lost his own grandfather not long ago and still missed him every day. He couldn't imagine how hard it would be for a child to cope with losing a parent so young.

Maybe this was a chance for him to help someone else whose life had been upended by tragedy, he thought. At least, he could try. "So, do you remember much about your father?"

"Some," Chase answered, spinning the ball in his hand before tossing it back. "He looked fine, but he was sick, and that made Mom sad. He didn't ever want to go outside or play games with me. She said it wasn't my fault, so I figured it was because he didn't want to be my dad anymore."

Laced with sorrow, those raw, honest words drove straight into Sam's heart. He'd assumed the Marine had died in combat, but now it sounded as if he'd made it home only to pass away later. Sam didn't know which was more devastating, but he suspected that to Holly and Chase, there wasn't much of a difference. Brady was gone, and they had to live without him. It didn't get much tougher than that.

It wasn't Sam's nature to delve into someone else's pain, especially since he had more than enough of his own to bear. But this brave kid and his grieving mother had broken through his stalwart front and gotten to him in a way other people didn't. Foreign as it was to him, he acknowledged that their heart-wrenching history made him want to do something to help them.

"I can't imagine that," he said. "You're a great kid, and I'm sure he was proud to be your dad. Sometimes when folks get sick it changes the way they act, even with the people they love most."

Unfortunately, Sam knew that from agonizing personal experience. His own family had taken turns supporting, coddling and spoiling him until their eggshell walking had all but driven him nuts. All but Brian, he reminded himself with a wry grin. His pain-in-the-neck younger brother had remained his usual difficult self through it all, scoffing when Sam pitied himself, knocking him back into reality when he needed it. Sometimes literally.

"Grown-ups are weird," Chase muttered, smacking the ball into his own glove with a scowl.

"Got that right," Sam agreed wholeheartedly, wishing he had some other form of wisdom to offer. But since he didn't, he opted to change the subject to something less depressing. "So, did you play on a team when you were in Boston?"

The boy's expression brightened like the sun coming out from behind a cloud. "T-ball, and then baseball."

"Nice. What position did you play?"

"I usually got stuck in the outfield 'cause I was the youngest."

His disgusted tone made it clear what he thought of that, and Sam chuckled. "What would you rather play?"

"Catcher. They're in the action all the time. The outfield's boring."

Sam couldn't agree more. Being in on every play was why he'd enjoyed the position so much when he was growing up. Chase's comments took him back to his own Little League days, and he chuckled. "Unless you get some gorilla up there who can hit the ball a mile. Then it's over your head and he's trotting around the bases like a big shot."

"Yeah, I hate that. If I ever hit a home run, I'll be cool about it."

"Whattya mean 'if'?" Sam demanded in mock horror. "Don't you mean 'when I hit a home run'?"

"It's pretty hard to do."

"Nothing worth doing comes easy." To Sam's astonishment, one of his dad's trademark sayings came tumbling out of his mouth. Even more surprising, it struck him as a very fatherly thing to say, and to his knowledge, he didn't have a paternal bone in his body. He liked kids well enough, but having his own was a faint dream, possibly in the distant future.

But somehow, he'd connected with this friendly boy in a way he'd never done with the rug rats in his own extended family. He wasn't at all sure that was good for either him or Chase, but now didn't seem like the time to examine it too closely.

Chase had been dropped into a new town, surrounded by strangers. For some reason, he seemed to enjoy spending time with Sam, and there was no point denying that the feeling was mutual. Out of respect for a fellow soldier who'd died too young, Sam decided that the least he could do was be around when his young neighbor needed someone to listen.

Or simply throw the ball back.

Holly was digging through a suitcase searching for some dry sneakers when she heard an odd sound out in the overgrown backyard.

Thwack, pause. *Thwack*, pause. The rhythm was steady, and she couldn't figure out what might be causing it. Then the sound of a deep voice, followed by Chase's unmistakable shout, "Awesome!"

Opening her bedroom door farther, she confirmed that he wasn't in his room but had somehow gone downstairs without her noticing. It wasn't smart for him to be wandering around on his own, and she made a note to remind him of the simple rules she'd established for him in Boston. Granted, Liberty Creek was a far cry from the city neighborhood they'd lived in before, but in her mind you couldn't be too careful when it came to your kid's safety.

Hurrying down the unfinished wooden stairs, she stopped dead in her tracks when she got a glimpse of what was happening outside the kitchen's bay window. Chase stood on one side of the ragged hedge, tossing a ball to someone on the other side. Technically, he'd stayed in the yard and was still managing to have some fun, and now that she knew he was okay, she admired his creativity with a grin.

Unfortunately, her humor was short-lived when she peered through another window and saw that his throwing partner was Sam Calhoun. Until now, she'd had no idea that he was one of Daphne's two neighbors, and she berated herself for not asking him where he lived.

Then again, she amended as she made her way to the porch, what were the chances that the former Ranger lived next door? She wasn't concerned about Sam harming Chase—he struck her as too compassionate for that—but she was very worried that her son might grow too fond of their troubled neighbor and suffer greatly for it later on.

So, when she reached the screen door, she summoned her most casual mom tone before saying, "Morning, boys. I didn't realize workouts started so early around here."

"Hey, Mom!" Chase greeted her, waving before lobbing the ball to Sam. "We're getting warmed up for the game tonight. Boston's playing the Yankees at Fenway, and we wanna be ready in case the Red Sox need us."

"His idea," Sam explained with a sheepish grin that was oddly endearing on such a large man. "I'm sure they'd be happy to get Chase in the lineup, but I don't imagine they'll need me unless someone breaks a leg going down the dugout steps."

In spite of her earlier concern, Holly couldn't keep back a laugh. "Let's hope it doesn't come to that, then. Are you two hungry?"

Typical boy, Chase whooped a reply, spinning his glove in the air before catching it and racing inside. She stepped back to avoid being run over and waited while Sam took a little slower route. His long strides crossed the yard quickly, and he set his battered glove on the top porch step before coming into the kitchen.

"You really don't have to feed me," he said. "I've got food at my place."

Just a few yards away, she noted silently, still a bit stunned by the way she'd uncovered that detail. But that wasn't his fault, and she decided to let it go. "You never charged us for those great cookies yesterday, so the least I can do is return the favor. How do you like your eggs?"

"However you're makin' 'em. When someone else is doing the cooking, I'm not picky."

"Scrambled it is." Considering his size, she added, "And some of that fresh local sausage I got yesterday, too. Anything else?"

"No, thank you," he replied in a cautiously polite tone. "That's more than enough."

She tried not to take the stiff response personally, but it wasn't easy. She was going out of her way to put her own misgivings aside and be friendly to him, but he seemed determined to shrink away from her efforts. It was probably for the best, she mused. From what she'd been able to discern, Sam needed a lot more than she could give him, anyway. "Okay, then. Grab some coffee and have a seat while I get everything ready."

He did as she asked, and she focused on putting their meal together. She could sense him watching her, and a quick peek showed her that he was following her movements with a thoughtful expression. Not creepy, she realized, but curious. She couldn't imagine what he found so fascinating about her cracking open eggs and flipping sausages, then decided that what he might be thinking was absolutely none of her business.

An old door sat across a cobbled-together base that wasn't much in the beauty department but was clearly standing in for an island to be built later. Leaning across the top, she called in to the den, "Chase, breakfast!"

"Coming!" He trotted in and fixed her with a hopeful look. "That new wild animal show is on. Can I eat in the den if I'm real careful?"

Her boy, Holly thought fondly. He loved anything with fur or feathers, and the wilder the better. "Okay, we'll give it a try. But keep your food on the coffee table and sit right in front of it. If you spill it, you clean it up. Understand?"

"Thanks, Mom. You're the best."

"Yeah, yeah, yeah," she grumbled with a mock scowl. "Save the flattery for when you're in trouble."

He laughed and turned to Sam. "Wanna come watch TV with me?"

Something flickered in the contractor's eyes, lighting them briefly before fading away. Holly got the impression that a part of him was trying desperately to claw its way to the surface but kept getting shot down by reality. Holly knew how discouraging it could be when the past kept smothering all your efforts to move forward, and she felt a pang of sorrow for him.

"Maybe next time," he replied.

"Tomorrow?"

Holly held her breath, praying that Sam wouldn't make a commitment and then not show up. Or forget. Or think it wasn't important. Or myriad other things that Brady had repeatedly done when Chase had attempted to reach out to him. Eventually, Chase had tired of being rejected and stopped asking his father to do things. Before long, Brady had become a stranger in his own home.

"I'd hate to say yes and then not be able to do it," Sam said quietly, as if he'd somehow picked up on Holly's unspoken fear. "Soon as I can, I'll watch that show with you. Is that okay?"

Chase nodded eagerly. "I get it. Mom says you should always keep your promises."

Apparently satisfied, he left the two adults in the kitchen, an awkward silence hanging in the air between them. Sam gave her a long, pensive look, as if he was trying to decide what to say next.

Finally, he told her, "That's good advice."

"I have my moments," she answered as lightly as she could, turning away to rotate the sausages before they burned.

"Good ones?"

"Mostly." At least now they were, she added silently. Getting to that point had taken every ounce of her strength, but she'd done it for Chase because she was all he had. Setting their plates on the table, she took the seat next to Sam and debated telling him the rest of her story. Because she believed that it was important for him to understand where she was coming from, she took a deep breath and started, "Sam, I don't normally do this, but since we're going to be seeing a lot of each other around here, I need for you to know something. About Brady."

Misery clouded Sam's eyes, and he grimaced so deeply, she almost felt it herself. Holly got the feeling that he wasn't only sad for her, but for himself. Whatever had scarred him had left a mark so deep, it showed as clearly in his features as if it had been chiseled there yesterday. "Chase told me about him while we were playing catch. I'm so sorry he didn't recover."

"Oh, he recovered," she corrected him with a frown. "Most of him, anyway. He kept on hunting for the rest, and when Chase was old enough to do things with, I thought being a dad might help him find what he'd lost. Sadly, it didn't, and two years ago, he finally gave up."

"That's awful. No family should have to go through that."

Sam's solemn response told her that he understood better than anyone what she and Chase had endured. In her experience, confiding in someone made them want to do the same, and she sipped her coffee, waiting for him to give her some idea of what had happened to him.

But he didn't.

Instead, he stood and pushed his chair back into place. "The ramp for Daphne's wheelchair came in this morning, so I'll be installing it first thing. It's gonna be pretty loud, but I'll get it done quick as I can."

"That's fine, but could you wait a few minutes? I really should check in with my parents. They were out last night, so I left them a message that we got here in one piece. They'd probably like more of an update, though, and I promised them some pics of the house."

"Sure."

Back to the single syllables, she noticed as he strode out the side door and headed down the steps that led to the driveway. Holly wasn't certain what kind of response she'd expected from the reserved contractor, but she couldn't help feeling that she'd fallen a huge step back where he was concerned. She'd taken a leap of faith to be honest with him, she reminded herself, and now she'd have to live with the consequences.

Whatever they might be.

Her laptop was charging on the counter, so she unplugged it and took it into the den, where Chase's show was nearly over. He swallowed the last of his orange juice while she dialed her parents in Savannah, and by the time their images appeared on the screen, he was grinning from ear to ear.

"Morning, Gramma and Grampa," he said, adding a little wave. "How're you?"

"Just fine, honey bear," Mom replied, beaming at him. "What have you been up to so far today?"

"Having breakfast and playing catch with Sam."

"Sam?" her father echoed warily. "Who's he?"

"Auntie D's neighbor," Chase answered brightly. "He likes the Red Sox, too, and he's awesome. We're gonna watch the game to-gether tonight."

They wouldn't like knowing there'd be a stranger in the house, Holly knew, but she plastered on a smile and pretended she was fine with the arrangement. Don Fredericks was a cop, and her mother, Gloria, worked with at-risk teens, so they were trained to spot trouble and she didn't want to worry them.

Unfortunately, Holly's acting skills left a lot to be desired.

"I didn't realize there was a single man so close by," Dad commented in a casual tone that did nothing to mask his apprehension. "I don't like the sound of that."

"Oh, Don." Mom clicked her tongue at him. "Daphne hired him to work on her house, so she thinks he's trustworthy. You know how great she is at reading people. Besides that, Holly meets new folks all the time, and she handles them just fine. Don't you, sweet-heart?"

"Sam's been a total gentleman," she assured them.

"Well, you tell him that better not change or he'll have your father to deal with."

"I'll do that," Holly promised, forcing a laugh. "He'll be too busy to cause any problems, though. This place is like something off one of those real estate disaster shows."

"D has always liked old things," Mom said in a tone laced with fondness for her older sister. "Now that she's retired, it's good for her to have a project that will keep her occupied."

"It'll do that, all right. I should let you two go for now. Once Auntie's home from the hospital, we'll call and have a nice family video chat."

"That would be wonderful," Mom said approvingly.

In unison, they said, "Love ya—bye."

After they hung up, Holly stared at the icons on her screen until they faded into a slideshow of Savannah's most beautiful spots. Sometimes her hometown seemed like it was on the other side of the world even though it was only a few hours away by plane. Those were the times when she seriously considered moving back to the only place that had ever really felt like home to her.

Brady had never wanted her to follow him from station to station, so she'd remained in Boston, counting the days from one of his leaves to the next. Enjoying her small circle of friends, she'd been happy enough there, even more so after Chase came along.

Then Brady returned, and their once-vibrant existence shriveled away to nothing. For Chase's sake, she'd done her best to adjust and remain as upbeat as possible. After trudging along that way for a couple of years, she'd finally come to the conclusion that Brady's condition had plateaued and the chances of him improving any further dwindled by the month.

So she cared for him as well as she could while creating a life for herself and Chase that included desperately needed friends and playdates. They'd been her salvation, giving her something beyond the confining four walls of their apartment.

Tragically, they'd also given Brady the opening he needed to end his life. For months afterward, she'd blamed herself for not being there when he needed her most, to remind him that she loved him and would never give up on him, no matter how bad things got. The vows she'd spoken on their wedding day before God and their families were sacred to her, and she was as committed to them at the end as she'd been in church that warm, sunny day that had held such promise.

It felt like a lifetime ago, she thought sadly. Every night, Chase included Brady in the prayers he said before bedtime, asking God to take good care of him. Because she felt he was too young to understand, Holly hadn't yet devised a way to tell her son the details of his father's untimely death.

She barely understood it herself, but she recognized that someday she'd have to tell Chase the truth. She prayed that when the time came, God would help her find the words.

And that somehow, her son would find a way to accept that the father he loved had chosen to leave him behind.

Later that morning, Sam stopped outside the kitchen door to find Holly and Chase with their heads together over a coloring book. He didn't think kids did that kind of thing anymore, and the cozy scene made him smile. "I'm headed into town for a fresh saw blade. Do you need anything while I'm there?"

Holly glanced over at her son and grinned. "I don't suppose y'all have a barber with a pair of hedge trimmers and a good sense of humor?"

"Aw, Mom," Chase whined. "My hair's fine."

"I can hardly see your eyes," she informed him in the kind of no-nonsense tone Sam recognized from his own mother. "Besides, it'll be getting warmer soon and shorter hair will be a lot more comfortable."

"Okay," the boy relented with a sigh. "Let's go."

They left the kitchen, and he waited on the landing with Sam while she locked the door. Then Holly took Chase's hand and they headed down the wide steps. When Chase reached out for Sam's hand, too, Sam was so stunned, he accepted the trusting gesture and followed along. That the boy would be openly affectionate with his mother was understandable. That he would think to include someone he'd known such a short time was surprising, to say the least. Their quick connection baffled him, but Sam decided that any problem he sensed was all in his mind.

His heart was overjoyed to know that the fatherless boy had taken to him so quickly. Maybe he wasn't as far gone as he'd feared, after all.

"So, is this barber good with kids?" Holly asked, giving her son's hair a fond ruffling. "This jack-in-the-box isn't great at sitting still while people fuss over him."

"Except when I was in the service, Hal's given me all my haircuts since I was five." She raised a suspicious brow, and he laughed. Since meeting the Andrewses, he'd been doing that more than he had in ages, and he had to admit it felt a lot better than brooding all the time. "I know I'm not much of an advertisement right now, but he's really good. He's got a grandson Chase's age, along with seven others, so he's great with kids and they love him."

"That sounds reassuring," she commented as they stopped beside her car.

To Chase, he said, "Cody, the one who's your age, came up with the idea of keeping a video game console and snack bar in the waiting room at the shop. I don't know who likes it more—the kids or their parents."

"What a fabulous idea," Holly said. "That's one smart kid."

"I wouldn't mind meeting him sometime," Chase said. "It'd be fun to have a friend to hang out with."

Remorse dimmed Holly's features, and she frowned. "I know you miss your old crew, bud. I wish we could've brought them with us."

"It's not your fault, Mom. I'll just make new friends."

After making sure she smiled, he grinned and climbed into the back seat of her car. Holly closed the door behind him and stared in at him with a pensive expression.

"That's one amazing kid you've got there," Sam commented.

Pulling her gaze away, she looked up at Sam. "He is, isn't he? I don't know what I'd do without him."

"I'm thinking he gets all that spunk from you."

Tilting her head, she gave him a long, penetrating look. "You think I'm spunky?"

He wasn't sure what was going on in that mind of hers, but he saw no harm in being up front with her. "Sure do. Considering all you've been through, you wouldn't have gotten this far without it."

"God had a lot to do with that."

Sweet and simple, the sentiment that comforted so many people made Sam's skin crawl, and he struggled to mask his reaction to her unexpected confession. He didn't quite manage it, though, and she frowned. "Did I say something wrong?"

"No."

"You look like I just sucker punched you." He didn't say anything, and after a few moments, understanding dawned in those expressive eyes. "You're not religious, are you?"

"Not anymore."

He waited for her to ask him why, but again this beautiful, perplexing woman surprised him. "So, where do I find this barbershop-slash-video-arcade?"

"If you want, you can follow me into town, and I'll introduce you to Hal."

"That sounds perfect. Thanks."

"No problem."

She flashed him the kind of smile that made him more than happy to interrupt his day and give her a hand. The midmorning traffic was lighter than usual, and they found two spots right next to a single-story brick building whose swinging sign out front said Hal's Barbershop. In the large windows, the owner had displayed posters of various hairstyles through the generations.

After commenting on the more humorous ones, the three of them headed inside. Bells over the door announced their arrival, and the familiar sound reminded Sam of his childhood. Clean and simple, the single room was painted a bright, welcoming shade of yellow, perfectly suited to the elderly man strolling through the rear door.

"May I help you?"

"I know we didn't call ahead," Holly replied, "but do you have a chair available?"

"I sure do." Offering his hand to her, he added, "I'm Hal Rogers, and I'd know Daphne's niece anywhere. And this young man," he said, grinning down at her son, "must be Chase. She talks nonstop about you when my wife and I play bridge with her at our place, so I feel like we're already old friends. What can I do for you?"

"Mom says I need a haircut," the boy answered in a disdainful tone that clearly said he didn't see what all the fuss was about.

Hal hummed, angling his head to examine one side of the kid's head and then the other. With a completely straight face, he asked, "Which one?"

When Chase laughed, Hal turned to Sam and said, "See? The classics always work."

"That's 'cause kids haven't heard 'em yet."

"I have, Papa, and I still like them."

Winking at a young boy reading in the waiting area, he said, "Thanks, Cody. It's always nice to have a fan. Have you met Chase yet?"

"No, sir." Without prodding, he walked over and offered his hand. "I'm Cody Rogers. Nice to meet you."

"I'm Chase Andrews."

"There was a half day of school today, so Cody's keeping me company while his parents are working," Hal explained, the fondness in his voice making it plain that he enjoyed the arrangement. "He's a big help around here, but once summer rec starts, I'll have to find myself another assistant."

"What's summer rec?" Chase asked.

"Beginning the last week of June, one of our teachers runs a day camp for kids from kindergarten through fifth grade." Hal went over to the front counter and took a flyer from the rack next to the cash register. Handing it to Holly, he continued, "They have it at the high school, so there's a pool and athletic fields for the kids to use."

"And a couple days a week—" Cody picked up the thread "—we have field trips. We go to an amusement park, go-kart track, mini golfing, stuff like that. This year we're gonna check out the new water park."

The excitement he obviously felt was reflected in Chase's expression, and he looked up at his mom with a hopeful expression. "That sounds like a lot of fun. Do you think I could sign up for that?"

"I don't know, honey." She stalled, flipping the paper over in an obvious attempt to buy herself some time. When she found what she was looking for, her eyes widened in surprise. "This is the total cost? For a whole month?"

"Yes, ma'am," the barber assured her, nodding. "The director knows folks around here don't have money to waste, and she wants to make sure they can afford some fun for their kids. It's especially nice since we had to close down our youth baseball program."

"What?" Sam broke in. "We've been running that league since I was a kid. What happened?"

"The usual," Hal answered with a frown. "We used the land as a favor from the owner. When a developer came through and offered him a small fortune for it, the league had to clear everything away so the acreage could be sold."

Bored from the conversation, the two boys ran off to play video games. But Sam couldn't focus on anything else. His mother and grandmother always made it a point to keep him updated on the goings-on around town, and Sam couldn't imagine how they'd managed to drop the ball on this one. Granted, he didn't always pay attention to what they were chattering about, but he definitely would have registered the fact that the baseball fields were gone. He and his buddies had just about grown up there, and knowing that they were gone was like a kick in the gut.

Aiming for a light tone, he casually asked, "How'd Gran and Mom miss that one?"

Hal's frown deepened, and he shot a hesitant glance Holly's way. Sam had quickly learned that she was more perceptive than most, and she smiled. "Don't mind me. I'll just go check out the snacks."

"You don't have to run off," Sam assured her before nodding to the barber. "Go ahead, Hal."

"It happened last year."

Sam felt as if someone had dropped a load of bricks onto his shoulders, and he searched for something coherent to say. The best he could come up with was, "Oh," and the sympathetic look on the older man's face made him want to crumple himself up and disappear.

He'd done plenty of that since coming home, and he'd gotten pretty good at it. But just as his heart began to sink, he felt a comforting hand on his arm. Looking into Holly's pretty eyes, he found something there he'd never thought to see again.

Understanding.

"Things get by us sometimes," she said gently, telling him that she could relate to the emotions he wrestled with every day. "The important thing is, how are we going to replace those fields? I can't imagine summer without baseball and softball games, and I'm sure most of the families around here feel the same way. There's a lot of wide-open spaces around Liberty Creek. There must be another plot of available land somewhere."

"My granddaughter Lynette was just start-ing to get the hang of that underhand softball pitching style," Hal added helpfully. "She'd love to get back into it over the summer, but the league over in Waterford is half an hour each way and costs twice what she used to pay here. With Cody in baseball and their younger brother in T-ball, their parents just couldn't swing the fees."

"They could use some coaches, too," Cody piped up, wandering into the conversation with Chase in tow. "Then we could have more teams."

"Sam would make an awesome coach," Chase suggested, throwing him under the bus without hesitation. "And since he was a catcher, he could help the pitchers get better." Turning to his new buddy, he made a sour face. "If yours are anything like ours were in Boston, they're really bad."

"Dude, you have no idea," Cody muttered.

"I'm not sure about that, Chase," Sam hedged, wary of making a commitment he wasn't sure he could honor. "Playing and coaching are two different things."

"Could you think about it?" the boy pleaded, eyes begging as much as his voice. "Please?"

It was tough to resist that face, and Sam finally relented a bit. "That I can do. And I promise that if I decide I'm not right for it, I'll ask around to see who else might want to help out."

"Okay."

The kid was obviously disappointed, and Sam felt like a complete heel. But in the end, he realized that declining was better than letting everyone down.

"Getting more kids to participate lowers the cost for everyone," Holly commented cheerfully, clearly trying to change the subject. "Our program in Boston worked well that way. The softball angle is a good selling point, since not all leagues offer it. If you get some parents to donate food, you can run concessions at the games. The supplies are free, so the money you make is pure profit."

"You sound like you know what you're talking about," Sam commented, not the least bit surprised. He'd quickly learned that this young military widow was easily one of the most upbeat, capable people he'd ever met.

"I was in the booster club for Chase's league the last two years."

"She was president," her son chimed in proudly. "We even had our names on our jerseys."

"We've got a good group here, too," Hal offered in a helpful tone. "Once the word gets around, I'm sure you'd have no trouble putting everything together."

"That's sweet of you, but I'd have no clue where to start. I haven't met anyone other than you, Cody and Sam."

"Sam can help," Chase suggested brightly. "He grew up here, so he must know everyone in town."

Two pairs of blue eyes swung to him, and Sam didn't have it in him to decline the way he normally would. "Kids should be able to play baseball, so I'll help out however I can."

She and Hal kept batting ideas around while Sam did his best to keep up. He got the distinct impression that he was being swept along by the wave of ideas, and he had a tough time following along.

But he liked it.

Once the awkward reference to his past had faded into the background, Sam found himself being drawn to the concept, knowing that it would be good for Liberty Creek and the hardworking families who lived there. They were the reason he'd enlisted in the Army years ago, why he'd trained so long and hard to become a Ranger.

He'd been devoted to protecting Liberty Creek and places like it, to keep the families who lived there safe from a world that seemed to be spinning out of control a little more every year. His service had left him battered in a way he'd never envisioned, but he'd always be proud of what he'd done for his country.

And now, a little boy was asking him to help in a different way. How bad could it be? Sam mused. He'd build a couple of dugouts, lay out some chalk lines, go cheer the kids on while they played. By the end of the summer, it would all be over, and he could feel good about being involved. This might be just the thing he needed to start feeling comfortable in his hometown again.

During a lull in the conversation, he screwed up his nerve and looked down at the boys. "I've got an idea for your team name. How 'bout the Liberty Riders?"

"Perfect," Holly said approvingly, smiling as if he'd solved a thorny problem for her. "It's got a nice historical feel to it, and we could work the bridge into the logo for their jerseys."

"I'll leave that up to more creative folks than me, but I'm glad you like it."

The two boys whooped excitedly, bookending him in a fierce hug that pushed him back a step. Looking over at Holly, he was rewarded with a dazzling smile that threatened to knock him the rest of the way off his feet. When she mouthed, "Thank you," the unspoken words hit him in a way that caught him completely by surprise.

Very firmly, he tamped down that unexpected reaction to his temporary neighbor. She and her son had been abandoned by a man who'd promised to care for them for the rest of his life. No matter how much he enjoyed their company, Sam was far too cautious to allow them to be hurt like that again.

At this point in his life, he'd reluctantly come to accept that while he was a lot better than he'd been, he still had a long way to go. It would be a tough slog for him, and he had no intention of dragging anyone along on that perilous journey with him.

Chapter Four

"Mom, please?" Chase begged, a juice box in one hand and a video game controller in the other. "Can I stay here with Cody?"

Holly wasn't at all sure that was appropriate, considering the fact that they'd just met the Rogerses. Her son's freshly cropped hair accentuated his bright blue eyes, and the pleading look in them made her want to agree.

"I don't know," she hedged, glancing to Hal for a hint of how he felt about the unexpected invitation.

His broad smile eased her concerns. "He's more than welcome, Holly. Cody's a great sport, but when I'm with a customer, he gets pretty bored."

"Papa's the best," Cody told Chase. "When we play that racing game, watch out. He beats me every time."

Stalling, she looked at Sam, who grinned back. "Looks like you're outvoted."

"I guess so. When should I come back to get him?"

"No need to make a special trip. I close at six tonight, so I can drop him off at Daphne's when I take Cody home."

"Okay." She knew Chase would balk at a hug, so she settled for knuckling his shoulder. "Have fun, but behave yourself. You know my cell number in case you need me, right?"

Rolling his eyes, he rattled off the number just the way she'd taught him as soon as he was old enough to memorize it. "I'll be fine. Me and Cody will have a blast."

And with that, he and his new friend zoomed across the shop to resume their paused game.

She and Sam said goodbye to Hal and headed out the door of his shop. Holly hadn't had a free afternoon in so long, she wasn't sure what to do. Sure, there was plenty of arranging and organizing waiting for her at the house, but it was such a nice, sunny day, the last thing she wanted was to be cooped up indoors. "I hate to waste such a gorgeous day on chores. Any suggestions for what I should do instead?"

After a moment, Sam suggested, "We

could go scout a new location for those base-ball fields."

"Perfect."

With a slight bow, he opened the passenger door of his truck for her to climb up into the cab. The balmy air rushed by the open windows as they drove out of town, and Sam nodded toward the radio. "Pick something to listen to if you want."

"That could be dangerous," she teased. "What if I like opera?"

He slanted her a look, then the corner of his mouth quirked with humor. "I'll risk it."

Laughing, she decided that her best option was to flip through the presets, assuming they were for stations whose music he enjoyed. She bypassed the jazz and talk radio, and when she landed on a channel playing a country ballad, she was more than a little surprised. "You picked this?"

"They play other stuff, too," he informed her good-naturedly. "I like music where I can understand the lyrics."

"I'm with you on that one," she agreed, staring out the window as they made their way past the edge of town. The scenery that had intimidated her the other day struck her as lush and beautiful now, and she took in the view with a real appreciation for the wild beauty that surrounded Liberty Creek.

After years of always doing the responsible thing, it felt good to do something on the spur of the moment for a change. It was just what she needed, and it didn't escape her that Sam had been the one to think of it. Even though they'd known each other such a short time, he seemed to understand her in a way other new acquaintances didn't. Maybe the fact that they'd experienced similar tragedies gave him a unique insight about her.

Even though she'd vowed to remain friends with her aunt's handsome contractor, she couldn't help feeling that in doing that, she'd be missing out on the best part of what he had to offer. Pushing the wistful thought aside, she focused on the view outside the windshield.

"It's so peaceful and lovely out here," she commented. "I can almost imagine the original settlers finding this spot and deciding there was no way they could do any better. You must've loved growing up here."

"Yeah, it was nice. We grew up a few houses away from the bakery, so the three of us pretty much had free run of the place. When Gran was experimenting with new recipes, we were her guinea pigs."

"Do they still live here?"

"Emma does, but Brian's a couple hours away, and my parents moved to Waterford about five years ago."

"I'm guessing you're the oldest."

He slid a glance her way. "How'd you know?"

"You act like it, taking care of people the way you do. What are they like?"

Sam chuckled. "Like younger siblings always are. Brian is a pain, and baby sister Emma is the princess."

"I'm sure she loves you calling her 'baby.'"

"Not really. That's why we do it."

Holly clicked her tongue in disapproval. "Boys can be so mean. I'm glad I have sisters."

"Daphne has a photo of the three of you on the mantel in the parlor. Your dad must've had his hands full keeping the boys away from you girls during high school."

"He's a traditional Georgia country boy, so his technique was to be cleaning a shotgun or rifle when our dates showed up," she recalled, laughing at the memory.

Sam grinned over at her. "When you talk about home, your accent really kicks in."

"Sorry about that."

"No need to apologize. It's pretty."

Holly had never met a man as forthright—

or as mystifying—as Sam Calhoun. Was he a staid New Englander who told it like it was? Or was he a wounded soldier struggling to move beyond his painful history and get on with his life?

While she was mulling that over, he slowed and pulled over to the side of an open meadow. With no buildings in sight, the wispy grass was waist high, and she caught a flash of white as two deer bounded toward a nearby stand of trees. A lone hawk circled overhead, doing lazy loops while he hunted for his lunch. Quiet and unspoiled, it was as near to idyllic as any place she'd ever seen.

"There's some acreage here we might be able to use," Sam explained. "Wanna check it out?"

"Definitely." She moved to open her door, then stopped. Sam had made it clear that he liked doing the gentleman thing, and after years of fending for herself, she wasn't too proud to admit that she enjoyed the attention.

They waded through the field, weaving around saplings that had sprung up here and there. Sam kicked the ground as they went. "It's pretty flat for the most part. Once we bush hog it down a bit, we can bring a commercial mower in here to neaten it up. After that, a good rolling should even things out well enough."

"You sound pretty confident that the owner will let us use this," she pointed out as they sat on a section of tree limb that had fallen nearby. "Don't you need to ask first?"

"Nah. He's a pretty good guy."

That rare twinkle appeared in his eyes, and she laughed. "You own this land, don't you?"

"Granddad left it to me in his will, along with the house in town. He wanted me to have something to come back to when I left the service. It's ten acres with a stream and a nice woodlot out back. I never knew what to do with it, so it's just been sitting here since he died. When we were kids, we used to run our dirt bikes out here."

The flash of humor vanished as if it had never appeared. His voice trailed off into something barely above a whisper, and he was frowning at something she couldn't see. Then she understood why. "Does 'we' include a friend of yours?"

"Yeah," he answered absently, not looking at her. "My best friend, Nate Henderson. We were stationed together, but—" Grimacing, he shrugged his broad shoulders in a helpless gesture. After a moment, Sam glanced around their peaceful surroundings and quietly added, "He really loved it out here."

She understood all too well how that felt, to be in the middle of a pleasant moment and have a dark memory pop up from nowhere to ambush you. "Sam, are you okay?"

"Mostly," he answered somberly. When his eyes met hers, she saw a glint of determination in them that told her he was being as honest as anyone could be. Her heart went out to this brave man who was trying so valiantly to gather up the pieces of his life and meld them into something he could live with. Heaving a sigh, he said, "Sorry about that. Sometimes I wonder if I'll ever get past what happened over there."

"One day you will, when you're ready."

"You sound pretty sure about that."

"I am," she assured him. "It took me a while, but eventually I learned to accept Brady's suicide as a part of my life. Now that Chase and I are here, it's obvious that leaving Boston was the first step in moving toward what's coming next."

"Which is?"

"I don't know," she confided honestly. "But I'll figure it out, and you will, too. You've made a good start with your contracting business. And I know a little boy who thinks you're a hero. The everyday kind that stops what he's doing to play ball or watch cartoons."

"Chase is a great kid." Pausing, Sam added a wry grin. "I'm still not sure how he talked me into helping out with his team, though."

She laughed. "Easy. He gave you those big, begging eyes and asked, and you couldn't say no. He's a little ham, just like his auntie D."

To her relief, Sam chuckled. "Yeah, she's tough to refuse. That's how I ended up buying four different bathtubs for the master bathroom."

"That's our diva. Gotta love her."

They both laughed, and then Sam got serious again. "Thanks for listening, Holly."

"Anytime."

The following afternoon, Sam glanced up when Holly appeared on the back porch, cordless phone in hand.

"That was Auntie D," Holly said with an amused look on her face. "She's going bonkers at the hospital, so Chase and I are going to visit her."

"Didn't you just go yesterday?"

"Yes, but she's bored so we're going again. She's going to be there two more days, and I asked if I could bring her anything from home. She said to bring you, the granite and backsplash samples for the kitchen, and something called lava cookies."

"One of Gran's inventions," he explained with a chuckle. "They're kinda like thumb-print cookies, but she makes 'em with marmalade so she can pile it on and let it spill over the sides. Can't imagine why Daphne wants to see me, though. The samples are small, so you could take them in yourself."

"She wants an update, in person. You know how she is," Holly went on, wiggling the phone and smiling. "Even a phone call is too impersonal for her. When she first retired, she complained about missing her friends. I offered to show her how to video chat with people anywhere in the world, but she hates computers."

Actually, Sam agreed with his eccentric client on that one, but since Holly and Chase seemed to like the baffling contraptions, he kept his opinion to himself. Instead, he wiped his grimy hands on his jeans and realized that wasn't going to cut it. "Well, I'm fine with going along if that'll make her happy. I'll get cleaned up and we can stop by the bakery on our way to the hospital. How does fifteen minutes sound?"

"Like ten minutes more than we need," she

replied in a lofty tone, swiveling to head back inside and holler for Chase.

Holly's breezy manner made him grin as he strolled across the yard and through a break in the hedge to his own front door. Now that he thought about it, ever since she'd dropped into the bakery on that rainy afternoon, he'd been smiling more than he could recall doing in a long time. People had been trying to lift his mood for months without much success. Somehow, the plucky Southern belle had done it in just a few days.

Crazy, but true. The face staring back at him from the bathroom mirror looked younger than it had lately, more optimistic. It was as if Holly's determination to move on with her life had started rubbing off on him, showing him a path forward from the gloomy pit where he'd been stalled for so long.

His former shrink would have a field day with that one, Sam mused as he pulled out his phone and pressed the speed dial for his grandmother's number. She answered on the first ring, and he could hear the whir of a mixer in the background.

"This is a nice surprise. How's my boy doing today?"

Ellie Calhoun was five feet tall and couldn't weigh more than a hundred pounds, but she still called every one of her twelve grandsons *boy* in an affectionate tone that Sam found comforting. She had a way of making him feel that no matter what happened to him, she'd always be there for him with a patient ear and his favorite snack.

"I'm good. Sounds like you're busy."

"Never too busy for you, Sam. What did you need?"

"Do you have any lava cookies?"

Once he explained who they were for, she laughed. "I've got the cookies but they need lava. Daphne likes the raspberry best, so I'll whip up a couple dozen for her and have them ready when you get here. Anything else?"

"No, that'll do it. Thanks."

"You're welcome."

She air-kissed the phone in her usual goodbye, and he ended the call as he trotted down the porch steps and met the Andrewses by the shiny blue pickup parked in his driveway. "Ready?"

"Auntie D and cookies?" Chase said. "I'm always ready for them."

"I don't know where you put all that food you eat," his mother chided, shaking her head as he climbed into the cab's center seat. "At this rate, you'll be six feet tall when you start third grade in the fall."

"That'd make you the star of the basketball team," Sam commented as he pulled out onto the street.

"Cool," Chase said, looking around the roomy cab with a child's curiosity. "This is bigger than the truck you had yesterday. Did you get a new one?"

"Just a different one. My work truck's filthy and full of lumber, so I figured it was better to take this instead."

When Chase's eyes fell on the hardware dangling from the rearview mirror, they widened with interest. "Is that an Army medal?"

Sam berated himself for not thinking to remove it before they got in. But he seldom had passengers, and the few who rode anywhere with him knew his painful history all too well and would never even consider asking him about it. "Yeah, it is."

"My dad had one kinda like that," Chase said quietly, clearly understanding the significance. "We keep it on a shelf in the living room. What did you get yours for?"

Sam hesitated. He could have given the expected answer, because he had a similar award tucked away in his top dresser drawer. But he'd quickly grown to like the inquisitive boy, and while tempting, the idea of deceiving him just didn't feel right.

So Sam took a quiet breath and tried to keep his answer simple. "It belonged to Nate, a good friend of mine. This was his truck, too. I always admired it, and he told me that if he didn't make it home from where we were, he wanted me to have it."

Sam felt the weight of those words crushing him, and he tried desperately to shake off the sensation that had plagued him for so long. Sometimes it felt as if he'd been lugging it around forever. He recognized that he had a white-knuckle grip on the steering wheel, and he consciously forced his muscles to ease up.

"Did Nate like the Red Sox, too?" Chase asked.

"Chase," his mother cautioned him. "I don't think Sam wants to talk about this."

Usually, he didn't, but for some reason the innocent question made him chuckle. "Actually, he was a Yankees fan."

"And you were friends?" Holly teased with a light laugh. "Is that allowed?"

"It was tough when they were playing each other, especially in the postseason. But we made it work. He was a good guy," Sam added, grinning down at Chase. "I was the catcher on our high school team, and he was our best pitcher. Had a mean screwball no one in the league could even come close to hitting. You would've liked him."

Nate's faded Yankees cap was still folded up in the glove box, right where he'd left it. Sam almost mentioned that, then thought better of it. Most folks would think that was odd, or even slightly insane, and he didn't want Daphne's guests to worry that he was nuts. Why that mattered to him, he couldn't say. But it did, and he decided that it was best to listen to his gut.

If only he'd done that on the fateful day that had changed everything, he lamented. But he hadn't, and now he had to live with the consequences.

Ellie Calhoun was nothing like Holly had expected.

The way Sam had described his grandmother, she was a combination of Julia Child and Attila the Hun. Instead, she was a petite woman with sparkling blue eyes and a smile that could probably repel even the most determined set of clouds.

"It's so nice to meet you both!" she exclaimed, embracing Holly and then Chase, beaming at them as if they were two of her favorite people in the world. "Daphne just goes on and on about you two, so it's wonderful to see you in person."

Interesting, Holly mused. Aside from pictures and a general description of the area, Daphne hadn't offered up many details about the place where she'd chosen to spend her retirement. And the people? Nothing. It was as if Liberty Creek was some kind of secret she was keeping to herself, and Holly couldn't help wondering why.

For now, though, she focused on returning the warm greeting. "It's great to meet you, too. We appreciate you rushing a batch of cookies for Auntie D."

Ellie waved off the thank you. "It's nothing at all. I've always got cookies stacked up in the freezer, just waiting for folks who want them. Don't I, Sam?"

She slid a look his way, and Holly followed the motion in time to see him chewing something that he'd obviously popped in his mouth while they'd been chatting. A quick glance at Chase showed her that he'd done the same, and she laughed. "Really, guys? You could've asked."

Sam swallowed quickly. "We didn't wanna interrupt you ladies while you were talking. That'd be rude."

"Yeah, Mom. Besides, sneaking them is more fun."

Hard to argue with that, she thought with a smile. She'd been so worried about uprooting Chase that it was heartening to see him quickly fitting into their new surroundings. Slipping back into mom mode, she prodded, "What do you say to Mrs. Calhoun?"

"Thank you, ma'am."

"You're very welcome," she replied, ruffling his hair in a practiced gesture. "There's plenty more where those came from, so no harm done."

She added an understanding smile for Holly, and she relaxed a little. She was so accustomed to keeping a tight rein on her son in Boston that it might take her a while to adjust to the more laid-back attitude here in rural New Hampshire.

"Now, these are for Daphne," Ellie continued, setting a covered plastic cookie tray on the counter. Then she stacked another one on top. "And this assorted tray is for the nurses. I've no doubt she's a horrible patient, and I'm sure they've had their hands full taking care of her."

"And then some," Holly agreed with a laugh. She reached out to take the cookies, but Sam beat her to it.

When she opened her mouth to protest, he gave her that boyish half grin that erased some of the years from his weathered features. "Just go with it, Peaches."

"That was my childhood nickname," Holly clarified, not wanting Ellie to think that she allowed men she barely knew to give her cute nicknames. Then she glared up at Sam. "Only Auntie uses it anymore."

"Got it." The grin deepened just a bit, and she caught a glimpse of a playful twinkle in his eyes that mimicked the sparkle she'd noticed in his grandmother's. It suggested to her that somewhere under all those scars was a boy who could still see the good things going on around him. It gave her hope that Sam could dig his way out from under the unspoken tragedy he'd suffered and have a happy life.

Of course, she wouldn't be there to see the changes, she reminded herself. It was just nice to believe they were possible.

Walking ahead of them to open the door, Ellie said, "Give my best to Daphne, now, and tell her we're all dying to see her when she's feeling better."

"We'll definitely do that," Holly promised. "Thanks again."

Leaning in, Sam kissed Ellie's temple on

his way by. She caught his cheek and drew his ear in to whisper something that made him smile. A real one, Holly noticed curiously, not the self-conscious kind she'd seen up until now. And despite her determination to keep him at a distance, she couldn't help wondering what Ellie had told him to get that kind of reaction.

Once they were back in his truck, he pulled away from the curb and headed for the highway. "She said she was proud of me."

"I didn't ask."

"Very loudly," he responded in a light tone that sounded almost like teasing.

"What's she proud of you for?" Chase asked in that abrupt way young boys did.

"For doing a good job on your aunt's house." Sliding a glance at Holly, he added, "But mostly for being her boy. I'm thinking your mom understands what that means."

"But you're a grown-up," Chase argued, his forehead puckered in confusion. "Why does your grandma call you her boy?"

"'Cause she does," Sam replied with a chuckle. "I kinda like it, actually."

"She's real nice, and she makes great cookies."

The kid logic made their driver smile, and Holly found herself joining in. She adored her son, but she'd always assumed that she was slightly biased. It was fun to see him interact with other adults and watch them respond to his sunny personality the same way she did.

The twenty-minute drive to the hospital passed by quickly enough, and when they reached the hallway that held Auntie D's room, Holly heard a familiar voice.

"But you don't understand. I don't want it that way."

She didn't catch the muted, professional reply, but it led them to an open doorway and a scene straight out of a TV sitcom. Her aunt sat at an incline, clutching the remote that adjusted the bed. Apparently, she wasn't sitting in the position the nurse thought was best for someone recuperating from a serious back injury, and they were literally fighting over the controls.

Face set in the fractious expression of a woman accustomed to having things precisely her way, the screen legend had stopped arguing but clearly had no intention of surrendering.

That's our D, Holly heard her mother's voice saying in her memory. *Sweetness mixed with hurricane. You might as well just give in because she never will.*

Summoning a light tone, Holly entered the

room and gave the nurse a sympathetic smile. "I'm Holly Andrews, Daphne's niece. Can I help somehow?"

"Ms. Mills needs her rest, but we're having a difference of opinion on how much."

The answer was delivered in a calm, rational tone, and Holly admired the woman's nonjudgmental attitude. Of course, in the break room later on, she wouldn't be surprised if it was a different story entirely.

"Holly, I've tried to explain—very nicely— that I don't require much sleep. She refuses to listen to me."

"She's the pro here, Auntie. Don't you think—"

"There's my handsome little man!" Daphne interrupted, motioning Chase over to the bed. The gold and diamond rings she wore clashed with the utilitarian hospital bracelet, but she didn't seem to notice. "Seeing you just makes my day."

"Careful, bud," Holly warned, pleased when he gently hugged their troublesome patient.

Then Daphne's eyes lit on Sam, brightening with unabashed joy. "Are those my lava cookies?"

The nurse opened her mouth to protest the illicit treats, but Holly lifted a brow in warning. After a moment, the woman nodded and left them with instructions not to tire out their patient.

"Please," Daphne huffed indignantly. "Tire me out. These people act as if I've got one foot in the grave. I'm bored out of my skull and so thrilled to see the three of you, I could positively bust."

The charming Georgia accent that had won her so many roles in Hollywood was on full display while she regaled them with the saga of her hospital stay. No mention of the accident that had put her there, Holly noticed. It proved how much her aunt thought of Sam that she'd go out of her way not to risk hurting his feelings by treading on sensitive ground.

"Are those the kitchen material samples you brought?" she asked in the voice of a child anticipating a treat.

"All ten of them." Sam set them on the tray beside the bed and wheeled it over for her.

She eyed each one carefully, tilting her head this way and that before sighing. "I can't decide. Holly, you've always had excellent taste. What do you think?"

It was flattering to be consulted, and she studied them before pulling two darker ones away. By process of elimination, she settled on what she believed was the best combination of backsplash and granite colors. "These will look nice in the sunlight and also when it's darker at night. Especially if you go with the ivory French country cabinets in this brochure," she added, flipping the designer catalog open to the right page.

Daphne angled her gaze to Sam. "She's good at this, isn't she?"

"She sure is."

He didn't sound the least bit surprised by that, and Holly barely resisted the urge to hug him. Daphne considered the samples, tapping her chin with a perfectly manicured coral nail. Then, to Holly's amazement, the retired diva looked her dead in the eyes and said, "You're hired."

"Excuse me?"

"You know my preferences as well as I do, and I have the worst time making decisions about any of this. I like each option better than the last one, and every change makes the project go on longer."

Holly laughed. "I seem to recall hearing something about four bathtubs."

"I'm not on a deadline, but I'm sure Sam would like to finish my house sometime this year, and me constantly changing my mind is only slowing him down." Looking at him, she went on, "What do you think?"

"I'd be happy to get some help with the

design end of things. I'm more of a hammer-and-nails kinda guy." Pausing, he gave Holly a little grin. "So welcome aboard."

"That's settled, then," Daphne said, brushing her hands together as if shedding herself of the problem. And then, she turned to Holly with pleading eyes. "But you need to take me home, Peaches. I'm going absolutely bonkers in here."

"You make it sound like you're in prison," Holly chided her. "You're only here for a couple more days, and from what I can see, you've got it pretty good."

The private room was large and sunny and filled to near bursting with flowers, balloons and cards from so many friends, Holly couldn't have named them all if she'd tried.

Folding her arms in a dangerous pose, her aunt clearly announced in an imperious tone, "I want to go home."

"We came in Sam's truck," Holly argued, glancing to him for some backup. "It's a long drive, and with your back in the shape it's in, you wouldn't be comfortable."

Daphne's deep blue eyes swung to her contractor, who suddenly seemed to be lacking a spine. Giving her an indulgent smile, he said, "I'll drive back and get your car. You can visit with Chase while Holly takes care of the paperwork. We'll have you outta here in no time."

And just like that, Holly's nice, orderly plan for preparing the house for Daphne's homecoming went out the window.

Chapter Five

One sunny morning, Sam turned at the sound of a familiar engine coming up the road. When a 1920s-era Ford turned into Daphne's driveway, he picked up a rag to wipe his hands and strolled out to greet her visitor. In the driver's seat was a man whose silver hair did nothing to dull the gleam in his hazel eyes. Sam didn't know how old Oliver Chesterton was, but he'd been the mayor of Liberty Creek for as long as Sam had been alive.

"Morning, Oliver. We've missed seeing you around here. How was your granddaughter's Parisian wedding?"

"Posh and pretentious." He made a sour face. "I would much rather have spent the last two weeks here, believe me."

Sam took the hint and moved on to more

pleasant topics. "It's nice to see Sally out of sick bay and back on the road."

"Not half as nice as it is to be driving her again. Modern cars might be easier to maintain, but they have no personality."

Sam stepped in for a closer look at the mirror-finish burgundy paint. "Looks like Steve freshened up the color for you while he was doing her overhaul."

"He did. It wasn't cheap, but worth every penny, I'd say."

Nate's truck had suffered a few dings over the past several months, and Sam made a mental note to get an estimate on some light bodywork. He didn't have the cash for it now, but once Daphne's project was finished, he should be able to afford some minor repairs. "What brings you out this way?"

"Our lovely star, of course," Oliver replied as he swung open the heavy half door and stepped out. Reaching behind the seat, he brought out the largest bouquet of flowers Sam had seen outside of a florist. "How's she doing?"

"Demanding and ornery, with a heavy coat of sugar. Pretty much like usual."

Oliver chuckled. "That's good to hear. I was going to wait a while longer before coming over, but I've been dying to see her for myself. Do you think she's up to having company?"

"I'd imagine so."

"I haven't met her summer guests yet. Is there anything I should know?"

"This isn't like a board meeting," Sam assured him as they went up the completed front steps to the restored set of double doors. "You don't have to be armed to go in there."

"I'm so glad to be done with those things," Oliver grumbled while he settled the collar on his shirt. "*Armed* is the right word, believe me. All that posturing and maneuvering—I was only too happy to cash out my shares and pass the baton to my siblings. Now they hate each other instead of me."

The regret in his voice was hard to miss. Being from such a close, loving family, Sam couldn't imagine feeling that kind of bitterness toward any of his relatives. Apparently, even Oliver's huge stockpile of money couldn't buy him everything he wanted.

When they walked inside, they found Daphne sitting on the sofa in her cozy den, reading a mystery novel. Chase was stretched out on the floor with a toy magazine, and Sam was struck by how similar the two looked. Those Mills genes were pretty strong, he thought.

Daphne glanced up when he knocked on the casement, her face lighting up when she saw who had walked in with him. "Oliver! Did you come all this way just to see me?"

"And to deliver these," he replied, holding out the huge bouquet with an even bigger smile. "I assume you have a vase somewhere."

"The big ones are all packed away, but I'm sure Holly can find one. You're a total dear, but you sent a lovely arrangement to the hospital. These really weren't necessary."

He crossed the room and set the flowers on a side table before leaning in to kiss her cheek. "Flowers don't last long. Besides, knowing you, you donated them to the other patients on your way out."

She actually blushed, and Sam had to smother a grin. The dapper widower had been alone a long time, and from the time Daphne had arrived in Liberty Creek, these two had been an item. While Sam wasn't in a place for it himself, he still thought it was nice to watch two lonely people connect with each other like that.

"Well, I've gotta run into town and pick up a few things," he said on his way out. "I don't know how long I'll be gone, but I'll make up the time later today."

"You don't have to check in with me, Sam,"

Daphne assured him graciously. "There's no time clock here, and I trust you to do whatever needs to be done."

Her unquestioning faith in him felt good, and he smiled as he turned to leave. Holly came up behind him unexpectedly, and he just about ran her down. She nearly lost her balance, and he braced her shoulders with his hands to keep her from falling. Once he was certain she'd regained her balance, he realized that he was all but holding her in his arms and took an awkward step back. "Sorry—this carpet's so thick I didn't hear you come in. Are you okay?"

"Since you rescued me, I'm fine. I didn't mean to startle you."

He used to be acutely aware of his surroundings, but lately that hypervigilance had begun to fade, and he'd dropped to a more normal level of awareness. When it occurred to him that they were all waiting for him to say something, he said, "It's not a problem. As long as you're okay."

Tilting her head, she smiled up at him. "Just fine. Honest."

"Sam?" Chase tugged at his arm until Sam looked down at him. "Could I go with you?"

He wasn't sure about it, but Holly gave him a subtle nod that told him she was fine with the suggestion. Studying Chase for a moment, Sam made a rotating motion with his index finger. "Let's get a better look at you."

The boy spun slowly, then came back to Sam with a hopeful expression. "I'm stronger than I look."

"I guess we'll find out, won't we?"

"Yup."

The kid was so upbeat about everything, Sam mused as they said their goodbyes and went out the kitchen door to his truck. It was too bad people couldn't keep that happy-go-lucky nature as they got older.

Maybe that was why he enjoyed spending time with his neighbor's nephew. It reminded him of a time when things were simple and easy, when the biggest problem he had was whether to walk to school or ride his bike.

He'd give anything to go back there, even for a little while. But everyone had to grow up sometime.

"Now, be careful," Holly warned Chase, who stood with his hands on the grips of Daphne's wheelchair Sunday morning. "This isn't a race or a chance for you to show off what kind of tricks you can do."

"You're absolutely no fun at all," Daphne scolded. Aiming a look over her shoulder at him, she went on, "We've been working on our wheelies, haven't we, Chase?"

"Your—" Holly started winding up for a good old-fashioned dressing down, then eased off when she caught the impish glint in her aunt's eyes. No wonder these two got along so well, she mused fondly. God had fashioned them from the same mischievous blend of characteristics. "Very funny. Now that I've recovered from my heart attack, can we please all just go to church?"

As if in reply, someone knocked outside, and she turned to find Sam framed by the kitchen's screen door. As if that weren't enough, his freshly pressed trousers and button-down shirt had a decidedly business-casual look to them. Not at all what he normally wore, and she let him in with a grin. "Wow, you clean up nice. Headed off to a business meeting somewhere?"

"Kinda," he parried with a grin of his own. "Thought I might tag along with you guys this morning. If that's okay."

"We're going to church."

"I know."

There wasn't even a beat of hesitation in his voice, and his calm, steady gaze was a warm blue color she'd definitely enjoy seeing more often. Behind her, she could sense the heightened interest of her family in the unusual scene, and to avoid having them ask any personal questions, she quickly answered, "Then we should get going."

In response, he pushed the door open, allowing them all to leave ahead of him. Then he pulled out his keys and locked the door behind them. It was the kind of thing the head of a family would do, and seeing it from him rattled her just enough that she stopped at the bottom of the ramp and stared at him.

"Can't be too careful, even in Liberty Creek," he explained, strolling down to join them near the car. Turning to Daphne, he offered his hand as if he was the gallant leading man in one of her films. She beamed up at him and let him settle her into the back seat, no fuss, no bother.

"Whenever I try to do something like that," Holly muttered to him while she opened the trunk to stow the collapsed wheelchair, "she fights me tooth and nail every step of the way."

Sam chuckled as he slammed the trunk closed. "I'm a guy, so it works better."

"I suppose. Plus, she likes you."

"Good to know." Turning to Holly, he gave her blue dress and ivory heels an approving once-over. "You clean up nice, too."

"Stop it, now. All this flattery will go straight to my head." He laughed out loud, something she'd heard from him so rarely it startled her.

Her reaction must have shown on her face, because he stopped abruptly and said, "You're looking at me like I've got two heads."

"It's just good to hear you laugh that way, is all."

"It feels good to me, too," he confided as he walked her toward the front passenger door. "I've spent a long time living in the dark."

Poignant and brutally honest, those words drove into Holly's soft heart with a swiftness that nearly knocked the breath out of her. His confession gave her a new perspective on what Brady had suffered through and just how difficult the end of his life had been. Staring up at him, she quietly asked, "Is that really how it feels?"

"Yeah." Reaching out, he gently brushed a stray curl back from her cheek. "But I'm coming out of it now, thanks to you."

"I didn't do that much," she protested, horrified by the thought of this courageous but still-recovering man coming to rely too heavily on her.

"I know, but you did the right things. I've

got a ways to go still, but you got me started. I'll always be grateful to you for that."

His voice had a cautious edge to it, and she realized that it mirrored her own anxiety. She hated to dash his hopes, but she wanted to make sure he understood that there wasn't a chance for anything romantic between them. Hoping she sounded sympathetic, she said, "Sam, Chase and I will be staying here just for the summer. Then we're heading back to Boston."

"I know," he echoed with that half grin that was beginning to grow on her. "I wanted to make sure I said my piece before you go."

"Okay, as long as we're clear on where we stand."

"Crystal."

She heard no bitterness in his tone, and his eyes hadn't lost the summery luster she'd admired earlier. So she smiled and slid into the soft leather seat, relaxing back into the kind of luxury she wouldn't mind becoming accustomed to.

Daphne put down her window, and as they drove toward the church in the square, she waved at her friends, who called out her name and waved back enthusiastically.

"It's kinda like traveling with the queen, isn't it?" Sam murmured to Holly as he turned into the parking lot that was already near capacity. Fortunately, a handicapped spot was available near the front doors, and he expertly docked the large, elegant car that Daphne had dubbed "The Yacht."

"You have no idea." She cast a fond gaze back at the loving, generous woman who'd shown her so much of the world. "Daphne Mills never met anyone she didn't want to know better, and they all feel the same about her. It's the most incredible thing you ever saw."

"I don't know about that," he said, giving her a look that finished his compliment without him speaking another word.

Holly felt her cheeks warming and focused on reaching back to fix Chase's collar to give herself a reprieve. She wasn't used to being admired, and certainly not by a man as impressive as this one. Military man, helpful neighbor, stalwart friend—there was a lot to admire in the tall contractor. A girl could do worse than losing her heart to Sam Calhoun.

Even before the last thought had fluttered through her mind, she dismissed it as foolish nonsense and mentally shooed it away. She had a son to raise and a future to plan. She didn't have the time or the energy for anything that would distract her from rebuilding the life that had been stuck in a holding pattern for far too long. No matter how handsome that distraction might be.

By the way people were reacting to Sam's presence in the quaint white chapel, it had been a while since he'd attended services there. Members of the congregation made a point of stopping to say hello, shake his hand or even embrace him. It was as if he was coming home again, and judging by the bewilderment on his face, that was how he felt, too.

"I see most of these folks all the time," he murmured as he guided Daphne's wheelchair toward a cluster of open seats in the back. "I don't know what's gotten into them."

While her aunt proudly introduced Chase to the folks seated nearby, Holly said, "They're happy to see you back in church. I think it's nice of them to make a fuss."

"Speaking of a fuss." Chuckling, he nodded toward a lovely young woman hurrying toward them from the front row. She was wearing a cute upturned white hat, and as she got closer Holly could see that it was meant to disguise the fact that she was completely bald underneath.

When she arrived, her short run had left her out of breath, and Sam frowned as he caught her arms to steady her. "Okay?"

She nodded gamely, gulping some air before bathing him in a delighted little girl's smile. "It's so awesome to see you! I've been praying you'd come back."

"Well, here I am. Holly and Chase Andrews, this is my baby sister, Emma."

"I really hate it when he and Brian call me that," she complained, even as she extended a slender hand to Holly. "I've been dying to meet you so I could thank you in person."

"For?"

Emma sent her much-taller big brother an adoring look. "For making Sam smile again."

Holly snuck a glance at him, wondering how the reserved contractor would respond to such a personal comment. Fortunately, he seemed to take it in stride and grinned back. "Reading sappy romance novels during chemo again?"

"Gran bought me a whole box of them at the library sale last month. They're the best distraction ever invented. They keep me from staring at the clock, waiting for my session to be over. It takes for-ever."

She stretched the description out in a way that reminded Holly of Chase. She'd never known anyone in treatment for cancer, but Emma seemed perfectly comfortable discussing it, so she reached into her old bag of hospital conversations for something to say. Noticing the filigreed silver-and-amethyst dangles bobbing from Emma's ears, she said, "Those earrings are really pretty. I've never seen anything quite like them."

"And you won't," she replied proudly. "I made them myself. Some of the other patients want me to make them jewelry, too, and I've started doing a few pieces at a time. Chemo can make you feel ugly, so it's nice to have pretty things to balance it out."

Emma's positive attitude was inspiring, and Holly recognized Sam's unrelenting determination in his younger sister. "How are things going?"

"Slow but fine," Emma replied in a bright, chipper tone that matched the whimsical hat she wore. "We'll know more in a few months. But I mostly came over to invite you, Daphne and Chase to lunch at Gran's. And Sam, of course." She lifted an expertly penciled-in brow at her brother. "Since it seems he finally decided to take a day off. Brian's here for the day, and with Mom and Dad still out in Montana, Gran thought we could all use some family time. And a decent meal," she added with a giggle.

"I'm not working at Daphne's," he explained, mischief glinting in his eyes, "but I've got other things to do. What're you having?"

"Come by the house and find out," she told him, flouncing a delicate shoulder as she sashayed back to rejoin the rest of her family.

Sam's protective gaze followed her until she was safely seated. As she picked up a hymnal, he sighed. "Man, I'm really worried about her. I wish she'd slow down a little."

"Some people do best when they're busy," Holly reminded him as they sat down in the row behind where Daphne and Chase had settled. "It keeps their minds off how terrified they are."

"Sounds like the voice of experience."

"That's because it is." Smiling, she nudged her son's shoulder. "One foot in front of the other, right, bud?"

Turning, he explained to Sam, "That's the first song I learned. It's from my favorite Christmas movie."

"*Santa Claus Is Coming to Town*," Sam commented, grinning at the boy's obvious surprise. "I liked that one, too."

"I thought it was cool how he could do stuff the animals did and how he was nice to people for no reason."

"Yeah, Santa's a good guy."

Chase gave him a long, curious look. "You know he's not real, right?"

"No way." Sam's jaw fell open in a shocked expression that nearly made Holly laugh out loud. "Are you serious? No one ever told me that."

Clearly not fooled, Chase rolled his eyes and shook his head. "Auntie D calls that over-acting. It's pretty funny, though."

"Kid's too smart for his own good," Sam muttered to Holly, who had to admit there were times she agreed with him. "You've all been invited to my grandmother's house for lunch after church, if you're not busy."

"What's she having?" Chase asked, making them all laugh.

Sam laughed, holding up his hand for a high five. "Good idea to ask first. The other day I think I heard her say something about Yankee pot roast."

The young Red Sox fan screwed up his nose in obvious disapproval, and Sam laughed again. "It's just the name some woman gave her recipe a long time ago. She didn't know any better."

"She probably wasn't a baseball fan."

"Probably not."

Fortunately, their mild female-bashing was cut off by the organist playing the opening chords of "How Great Thou Art." Holly was a passable alto, but she was more than a little impressed by the tall bass standing next to her. Chase's voice wandered through the chords, landing on an accurate note here and there. His efforts earned him an approving smile from Daphne, and once he took his seat again, she reached over the arm of her wheelchair to hug him briefly.

Up front, a man dressed in a simple gray suit strolled from his spot in the tenor section of the choir to stand behind a simple lectern at the front of the aisle. Sunlight streamed through the tall multipaned windows, brightening the age-darkened oak interior of the small church. The bottom sections of each window tilted in, allowing the sounds of birds inside. Holly had been in more impressive houses of worship, but none gave her the feeling of peace that she felt inside this quaint New England chapel.

Pastor Brown shuffled some papers on the lectern, frowning at the contents before folding them and tucking them in the interior pocket of his jacket. Resting his arms on the slanted top, he folded his hands and smiled at the congregation. "I think I'll save that one for another time. You don't mind, do you?"

Everyone laughed, and after they quieted

down, he continued, "Early this morning, I was out in our garden, marveling at how plants come back year after year. During the winter, they go dormant, waiting for the right time to bloom again. Sometimes, the same kind of thing happens to people."

Holly felt Sam stiffen beside her, and while the preacher didn't look directly at him, she guessed that the former soldier knew exactly who this particular message was intended for. She couldn't tell if he was pleased to be included in the impromptu sermon, but judging by his reaction, she suspected that he'd rather not be singled out this way.

"Life takes twists and turns that none of us can foresee. Some are wonderful, like falling in love." Pausing, he smiled over at the choir director, who beamed back as if they'd just met yesterday instead of many years ago. Turning back, he frowned. "Some are horrible, and they challenge our resolve in ways that make us wonder if we can ever recover. In those times, our own strength isn't enough to get us through. Fortunately, there's someone watching over us who's always there for us to lean on. All we need to do is put away our pride and ask Him for His help."

Without a word, Sam stood and stalked from the church.

As she watched him go down the steps and turn onto the sidewalk, Holly realized just how difficult it had been for the former soldier to put aside his lingering anger and give God another chance.

Sam's brave effort couldn't have ended any worse, and she wondered if he'd ever be able to find his way back.

Sam was sharpening the blade for his table saw when a shadow appeared in the open doorway of his garage workshop. He didn't have to look up to know who it was, and he growled, "Go away."

"We missed you at lunch," Holly said, ignoring his terse order and invading his workspace. Leaning against a hand-hewn beam that held up the roof of the old carriage house, she didn't say anything more. He figured that if he stayed quiet long enough, she'd take the hint and leave.

But she didn't.

After several minutes of stubborn silence, he finally angled a glare over at her. He'd been expecting disapproval, at best, so what he saw instead surprised him. Sadness clouded her beautiful eyes, and something in his chest tightened at the thought that he'd been the one to put it there. While he wasn't accustomed to explaining himself to people, after all she'd done for him, he felt as if he owed her some kind of reason for his odd behavior.

The trouble was, he didn't have one. So he went with the truth. "I just couldn't stay, Holly. I tried, but I couldn't do it. I begged God for His help that day, and Nate still died."

"I know."

"You're the only one who does," he reminded her as calmly as he could manage. "I wanna keep it that way."

She gave him a long, assessing look. "For how long?"

"I don't know," he snarled, losing the precarious grip he'd had on his temper all day. Recognizing that none of this was her fault, he dredged up a more civil tone. "So, how was your pot roast?"

"Delicious, of course. Ellie told me she's really proud of you for the step you took today."

"Not that it mattered."

"It did to her."

With that, Holly turned on her heel and walked out, leaving him staring at her back. Ramrod straight, it reminded him that the slender Southern belle had a backbone of pure steel, and even his worst mood didn't intimidate her in the least.

His family knew better than to tangle with

him when he went into what Brian called his grizzly bear mode, Sam groused silently, tossing tools into their trays and slamming drawers shut hard enough to shatter what had been a quiet Sunday afternoon. Far from helping, the tantrum only ratcheted his frustration higher.

Desperate to escape from it, he briefly considered taking Nate's truck out on some back roads before reason kicked in to warn him that was a very, very bad idea. Driving in his current state, he could hurt himself or, worse, someone else. Casting around for another solution, his gaze fell on an old ax leaning in a corner. Draped with cobwebs, it suggested just the kind of manual labor he was looking for, so he grabbed it and headed for Daphne's jungle of a backyard.

At least this way, he wouldn't be a menace to anyone but himself. And any unfortunate trees standing in the way of the Japanese garden Daphne had admired in one of her magazines and promptly decided she wanted.

He had no idea how long he'd been at it when he heard the back door open and then close. Feeling much calmer now, he paused and glanced over to find Holly picking her way through the waist-high grass and thistle bushes, plate in one hand and the handle of a large thermos dangling from the other.

Realizing he must be a total mess, Sam reached into the back pocket of his jeans for the bandana he habitually carried. But today it wasn't there. Exasperated and fuming when he left his place, he'd been too preoccupied to think of grabbing a clean one.

After setting the food down on a nearby boulder, Holly sat next to it and handed him the dishcloth she'd draped over her shoulder. "I thought you might want this."

This woman had an uncanny ability to think ahead, and he took the towel from her with a sheepish grin. "Thanks."

"You're welcome. I figured you must be thirsty, so there's ice water in the thermos. I don't know what kind of sandwiches you like. I hope ham and cheese is okay."

"It's great. Thank you." Mention of food reminded him that he'd missed lunch, and his stomach growled insistently while he wiped his face.

Apparently, it was loud enough for her to hear, because she smiled. "Sounds like I'm just in time."

"You seem to have a knack for that."

"Taking care of Chase keeps me on my toes. And now, there's everything to do here besides. Being organized is the best chance I have of not losing my mind on a daily basis."

"I can just imagine."

Looking around at what he'd accomplished so far, she asked, "So is this where the Japanese garden is going to be?"

"Only if you like this spot."

"I do," she assured him immediately. "It's exactly what I had in mind."

If he hadn't seen it for himself, he'd never guess that this calm, composed woman had been irritated enough with him earlier to storm out of his garage in a huff. Sam wasn't sure if that meant she'd decided not to give up on him, or if she'd chosen to back-burner that incident for now. But he'd been raised to take responsibility for his actions, no matter how humiliating they might turn out to be.

Sitting on the ground to avoid towering over her, he looked up at her with what he hoped was a contrite expression. "Holly, I'm sorry for how I acted earlier. My reaction to the pastor's sermon wasn't your fault, and I never should've taken my frustration out on you."

"You're right." The blunt response made his heart sink, but then she surprised him by smiling. "But you're also forgiven. I know how it feels to be furious and not have anyone to blame."

"I blame God," he corrected her bluntly.

Her smile took on a melancholy character, and compassion softened her eyes. "That will change someday, when you're ready."

"You say that a lot."

"That's because it's true."

With that, she kissed his cheek and stood up to head back inside. While he wolfed down a meal he hadn't even realized he needed, her gentle advice echoed in his mind. Knowing that someone understood the baffling shifts in his mood was so comforting, it amazed him. While other people had shown him sympathy and patience, Holly could actually relate to what he was going through. So when she told him that he'd eventually work his way through it and out the other side, he believed her.

Somehow, Holly had broken through the barrier he'd built around himself and shown him that he could absorb his devastating past and still have a future. He admired the young widow's strength in picking herself up and moving beyond the senseless loss of her husband. Even more, Sam appreciated her being kind and tough with him at the same time. He didn't know how she managed it, but her faith in him made him want to prove to her that he was worthy of her confidence.

He finished off his sandwich, then leaned back to admire the sunny afternoon that had seemed so bleak to him earlier. A pair of goldfinches swooped in to perch on neighboring branches of a grand oak tree, squawking at each other while a squirrel scampered up the trunk and disappeared into a knothole. Butterflies floated through the tall grass, lighting here and there before taking off again.

Now he understood why Holly had insisted on putting in a garden this far from the house. Peaceful but far from quiet, it was the ideal spot for someone to go when they needed a little solitude. He was no landscape designer, but when he closed his eyes he could almost hear the bubbling of the waterfall and pond she'd sketched out for him to create.

Even though he'd been skeptical of the idea at first, now he got it. And if he had to dig every foot of the thing by hand, he'd make sure this turned out to be the most exquisite Japanese garden in all of New Hampshire.

Chapter Six

"Oh, just leave those," Daphne insisted as Holly started to clear the dining room table. Chase was upstairs, sprawled out on his bed in his clothes after a long day of boyishness that would have put her out of commission for a week.

Carefully sitting back in her chair, Daphne smiled. "We haven't had much time to chat with everything that's been going on. How are you and Chase adjusting to Liberty Creek?"

"We're fine," Holly hedged, unwilling to confide her growing uneasiness about the future. Chase was flourishing in their temporary circumstances, buoyed by the rambunctious herd of friends he'd made at summer rec. He seldom mentioned his old crew, which was a relief to her.

Her own situation wasn't quite as rosy.

Having spent the past couple weeks away from Boston, it had become more apparent that going back there might not be the best strategy to ensure her own happiness. Not to mention the fact that no matter what angle she came at it from, the solution to her career problem proved to be as elusive as ever.

While she didn't say anything more, Daphne was clearly not buying Holly's determined cheerfulness. Worry marred the face that had long ago been deemed one of the most beautiful in the world. Even without makeup to smooth the lines that had begun appearing, Daphne was one of the most striking women Holly had ever seen. It was her eyes, she suddenly realized. Violet blue and snapping with intelligence, they were trained on her now. Judging by her expression, they didn't approve of what they were seeing.

She wouldn't stand up to that kind of scrutiny for long, Holly knew. As if it sensed that she needed rescuing, the dignified grandfather clock that reigned over the upstairs hallway chimed eight times. "It's time for your medication. Why don't we get you settled in your room so you're comfortable when the muscle relaxers kick in?"

"All right," she agreed in a meek voice that was totally unlike her. It clued Holly into the fact that she was more than ready for some relief from the pain that still tended to catch up to her this time of day. While she helped Daphne stand, the woman's frailty struck her hard. Daphne had always been strong and independent, savoring the grand adventure that her life in the movies had given her.

Now, she needed Holly's help simply to stand. When their eyes met, she saw the fear in Daphne's eyes. It was sobering, to say the least, and she immediately panicked. "I should get your wheelchair."

"No, the doctor told me to walk as much as possible."

"I think you left your walker in the kitchen when we were making cookies earlier."

The consummate Southern lady let out a decidedly rude snort and straightened to her usual regal bearing. "Walkers are for old people."

That was the spirit she'd always admired, and Holly couldn't keep back a smile. "All right, but there's a new threshold between the tile and carpet, so keep a hand on my shoulder in case you trip."

It wasn't more than a few yards, but she held her breath until Daphne was safely in her queen-size bed. Once the pillows were set up behind her, she cocked her head with a little smirk. "See? No problems here."

Shaking her head, Holly handed off the medication and a glass of water. "You're determined to get an award for World's Worst Patient, aren't you?"

"Absolutely." After taking the medicine, she added, "But cheer up, Peaches. Once I'm on my feet again, you can get back to your own life."

Holly wasn't sure how to respond to that, since she really didn't have anything to go back to. She busied herself adjusting the blinds so the next morning's sunlight wouldn't wake her fractious patient too early. When she was satisfied, she picked up Daphne's cell phone and ticked her own number to make it first in the list. "I found an alert app online this morning and downloaded it to your phone. Hit my number and then this siren icon—" she demonstrated the impossible-to-miss alarm "—and even if I'm asleep, I'll know you need me."

"What?" Daphne teased, a playful glint in her eyes. "No bell?"

Despite the roller coaster of emotions she'd been riding, Holly couldn't help laughing. The welcome feeling dispelled some of her tension, reminding her of why she loved this woman so much. "This is the twenty-first century, so no. Are you set for now?"

As the strong relaxers began to take effect, Daphne closed her eyes and snuggled down into her bed with a contented sigh. "Mmm-hmm."

Holly waited until her breathing grew regular, then crept from the parlor and closed the door behind her. She took care of the dishes, then started in on the large stack of ironing. She hoped that if she focused on the mindless task, her tangled emotions would free up and she could work through her tangle of thoughts in a calm, grown-up way.

"Is something burning?"

Sam's unexpected question jerked her back to reality, and Holly was horrified to see wisps of smoke curling up from the iron. Pulling it away, she groaned at the burn on the pale pink silk. "Wonderful. I don't suppose there's any place around here that sells Chanel clothes?"

"Sorry." Leaning in, he murmured, "The good news is, I saw at least two more like it in her closet upstairs."

"Are you blind? They're peach and almond. This—" she waved the ruined blouse at him "—is blush."

He held up his hands in mock surrender. "Sorry. To me, they look pretty much the same."

"Pretty much the same isn't good enough," she informed him tartly. "Maybe I can order one online and get it here before she notices."

"Why not just tell her? She'll understand."

Tired and exasperated far beyond her normal endurance, Holly folded her arms and glared up at him for all she was worth. "Did you come in here to aggravate me or did you want something?"

"I wanted to warn you not to use the kitchen steps. I tore 'em out and won't have the new ones done until sometime tomorrow."

His news did nothing for her already sour mood. "I'm grocery shopping tomorrow."

"The front steps are fine."

"So I have to drag all that stuff through the entire house to put it away? If you'd asked me, I could have told you to wait one more day."

He heaved a tired sigh. "I could build some temporary ones, but I'd just have to rip them out later on. If you want direct access to the kitchen, it's probably better for you to use the ramp."

"You're kidding, right?"

"Look, Princess," he snarled, "I've had a long day, too, and I've still got more to do."

His nasty comeback set her teeth on edge, and any other day she'd have backed down with an apology. Today was way beyond the usual, though, and after holding her emotions in check all day long, she finally gave in to her temper. "Did you call me 'Princess'?"

"If the glass slipper fits, you might as well cram it on."

Holly's phone sang with Daphne's signature ringtone, which struck her as odd since the alert was easier to use. Struggling to regain control of herself, she paused their argument with a raised finger while she answered it. "Yes?"

"Put me on speaker, please."

"Why?"

"Because I said so."

That was the diva tone, the one a smart person never messed with. "Okay, go ahead."

"What on earth are you two arguing about out there? The Drummonds across the way can probably hear you."

Holly traded a guilty look with Sam. He shrugged, motioning for her to answer however she wanted. He could have ratted her out, blaming the noise on her being a demanding shrew, but he didn't. He was giving her the chance to explain it her way, she realized, rather than taking the opportunity to make it all her fault. Which, in retrospect, it kind of was.

"Sam's working on the kitchen steps," she

began, staring at him while she spoke. She noticed that his hair had taken on a sandy color, with lingering streaks of blond, probably from being outside so much lately. Usually, she picked up on things like that right away, but even though she saw him every day, the difference had escaped her until this evening.

"And?" Daphne prompted.

"And he offered to build some temporary ones before he leaves," Holly continued quickly, feeling foolish about losing her train of thought. "But it's late, and he's done so much already, I think he should go home."

Those blue eyes warmed to some color even a top-end designer couldn't properly describe, and she felt herself smiling back. Their childish battle forgotten, she mouthed, "Sorry."

He rewarded her with a grin that would have buckled the knees of any woman over twenty and still breathing. It was a good thing she knew better, or she'd have been in major trouble spending so much time with the handsome contractor.

"I agree," Daphne announced in an authoritative tone that allowed no room for discussion. "Sam, you're a dear, but we'll be just fine without those extra stairs. You go home and get some rest. That's an order."

"Yes, ma'am."

Apparently satisfied, she ended the connection, and the kitchen echoed with quiet.

"Tell you what," he said in a hushed voice. "I'll head home and knock together some steps, then bring 'em back and bolt 'em onto the porch so she doesn't hear me banging away out there. Shouldn't take more than a half hour, but they'll be safe to use."

"How do you plan to do all that in the dark?"

"Well, now, around here we've got these newfangled things called lights," he replied in a decent Southern-style drawl. "Maybe you've heard of 'em."

In spite of her grumpy self, Holly felt a smile quivering at the corner of her mouth and firmly pressed it down. "Are you making fun of the way I talk?"

"I like the way you talk," he assured her in his usual New Englander voice. "It's smooth and sweet, so it reminds me of maple syrup."

"It does?" She'd never heard it described that way, and she had to admit she didn't hate it. When he nodded, she teased, "That's good, right?"

"Seeing as I love maple syrup, it's very good."

After their earlier spitting match, she couldn't imagine why he was being so incredibly nice to her. But his forgive-and-forget approach worked for her, and she gave in to a little smile. "Thank you."

"No problem. Just keep Daphne in her room so she doesn't see me, or we'll both be in trouble."

Adding a wink, he strolled toward the kitchen.

"Sam?" He turned back, and she gave him a grateful smile. "I'm sorry I bit your head off. I know it's not an excuse, but it's been a really long day."

"I kinda figured that. Don't worry about it."

Flashing her an encouraging smile, he headed out the side door and down the ramp. She didn't know what she'd done to deserve his understanding, but she was really glad he'd chosen to cut her some slack. She definitely needed it.

"This baseball committee's really not my kinda thing," Sam muttered as he and Holly walked toward the bakery.

"I know, and if you hate it, you don't have to come again."

"Promise?"

She laughed, and after a moment, he joined her. He kept reminding himself that he knew all the people who'd volunteered to run the Liberty Creek Youth Baseball and Softball

League. The trouble was, they knew him, too, and he wasn't at all sure what kind of reception to expect from them.

"You're donating the land for our fields," Holly commented, as if she'd somehow read his hesitant thoughts. "Without you, there wouldn't be a meeting because there'd be no baseball this summer. Just remember that."

She had a point, and he felt himself relaxing in response to her pep talk. "Okay."

It was seven thirty, and the sign in the window read Closed, but he pulled out the original brass key and unlocked the door. The scent of fresh coffee and baked goods met them in the entryway, and he chuckled. "I told Gran not to fuss."

"I'm glad she did," Holly replied, clearly relieved. "Snacks always make a meeting go better."

Her comment was laced with unmistakable anxiety, which surprised him. She'd struck him as the competent, take-charge sort of person, so the glimpse of vulnerability was something new. Putting aside his own misgivings, he said, "You sound nervous."

"So do you." It could have been a shot, but her smile eased the bluntness with understanding. "I know this isn't easy for you, but I promise it'll be fine."

He couldn't shake the feeling that he should have been the one propping her up instead of the other way around. Then his grandfather's voice floated into his memory, and he smiled back. "Granddad used to say that courage was doing something even when it scared you to death."

That got him the reaction he was after, and her smile deepened to show a single dimple in her left cheek. "I'd say we're both pretty brave."

"Yeah, we are."

Gazing down at this extraordinary woman, he could feel the warmth of her drawing him closer. She represented everything he'd given up hoping for, and judging by the affection sparkling in her eyes, he knew he could have it if he just reached out and took it. He wanted nothing more than to gather her into his arms for a kiss, and he needed every ounce of his strength to keep the distance he'd committed to when they first met.

"Sam, are you okay?"

"Sure," he replied, taking a healthy step back before turning away from her. Shaken by the strength of his emotional response to her, he cast around for something constructive to do. "I'll set up a couple tables and some chairs while you get the food."

"All right."

Fortunately for him, she'd grown accustomed to his step forward, step back approach to everyday situations, and she seemed to be adding this one to the list. The simple task of arranging the meeting space kept him well occupied, and by the time other people began arriving, he felt more like his usual self.

Whether that was a good or bad thing, he couldn't really say.

Hal Rogers was the first one to greet him. "Good to see you, Sam. I've got some open time this week if you'd like to stop by for a trim."

The kindly grandfather had buzzed his hair before he headed off to boot camp and for years had refused to charge Sam for his visits to the barbershop. Running a hand through his shaggy hair, he couldn't help chuckling. "Guess I'm overdue."

"How does tomorrow at nine sound?"

"That'll work, but you have to let me pay you this time. Just like I'm any other customer."

Hal studied him for a long moment, as if he was trying to decide something. Finally, he gave in with a nod. "All right, then."

They shook to seal the deal, and Sam got the impression that something important had just happened to him. Then he realized that it was the first time someone who'd known him all his life had treated him as if he was a regular person, not a wounded soldier. The change might seem small to others, but to Sam it meant everything.

By eight o'clock, there were a dozen baseball parents—and a couple of grandparents—gathered around the tables, chatting and enjoying the refreshments Gran had left for them. When everyone seemed to be more or less settled, Holly stood up and waited for the conversations to die down.

"Thank you all so much for coming tonight," she began, sending a welcoming smile around the small crowd. "I don't want to keep you too long, so let's get started."

Organized as always, she handed out agendas and sheets for taking down people's contact information. "I like email and texting, but if you prefer hard copy and phone calls, please add that to your other info. Now that we have a location for our fields, we can get things in gear. This first season will be shorter than usual, but if we all pull together, I'm sure we can give our kids a fabulous season of baseball and softball. Now—" she spread her hands out in an open gesture "—let's hear your ideas."

There was no shortage of those, and Sam marveled at how she acknowledged each person in turn, jotting notes and encouraging quieter folks to speak up. They talked through the logistics of prepping the fields, advertising the new opportunity around the area and making sure they had the right liability insurance. She tagged the simpler suggestions for immediate attention and tabled more complicated ones—like electronic scoreboards—for future seasons. He was no expert, but Sam thought there were enough items on the list to carry the league for years to come.

After an hour of pretty furious brainstorming, Holly gathered the stack of papers and tapped them on the table efficiently. "This is a great start, everyone. Would anyone like to type these up and get them distributed in the next day or two?"

A young mother timidly raised her hand, and Holly rewarded her with the job and a brilliant smile. "You're a brave woman, Brenda. Thanks so much."

"It'll give me something to do while the baby's napping."

"Yeah, I remember those days," Holly responded with a laugh. "Enjoy them while they last."

The shyness left Brenda's delicate face, and

the discussion rapidly shifted to children and how fast they grew up. While Sam couldn't contribute anything, he didn't mind just listening for a while. Being sociable wasn't his style, but he found that he enjoyed being part of the friendly group that had decided baseball was important enough to forfeit some of their time.

And then, someone addressed him by name.

"Sam, it's so generous of you to donate the land we needed," the woman sitting across from him said. "How can we ever thank you?"

Panicked by the direct assault, he stiffened reflexively while his mind began spiraling, as if it was flailing for something to latch onto. Beneath the table, he felt a warm hand gently squeeze his, encouraging him to answer. Glancing at Holly, he saw that she was still writing on her notepad, even though she'd discreetly made the bracing gesture to bolster his confidence.

Grasping her hand gently, he tapped into her remarkable strength and did his best to smile. "Knowing the kids'll have fun out there this summer is thanks enough for me."

"Can I talk you into coaching the catchers?" her husband asked. "As I recall, you were quite the backstop in high school."

The innocent reference to his own baseball days came perilously close to mentioning Nate, and Sam took a deep breath to make sure his voice came out in a normal tone. "You were an All-State infielder yourself, Gary, so I'm sure you can handle any of the positions. But if you want an extra hand now and then, just let me know."

"Excellent. Thanks."

While they traded a couple of stories from their playing days, Sam felt some of the constriction in his chest loosen, as if some unseen fist had loosened its death grip on his heart. It was a simple thing, talking baseball with an old friend, but to Sam it was a huge step toward finding a way to be content in his hometown.

And it felt incredible.

Chapter Seven

After a long day of chores and chauffeuring people around, Holly groaned silently when she remembered that Daphne's bedding was still in the washing machine, and it was almost 7:00 p.m. On her way upstairs for fresh sheets, she poked her head into the den and found Chase curled up on the sofa beside Daphne, reading her a story about endangered animals living in the Amazon. She paid close attention, stopping him every few lines for questions that showed she was listening but were simple enough for him to answer. The sweet, cozy scene made Holly smile, and she left them feeling a lot more chipper than she had only a few minutes ago.

In the master bedroom, she snapped on the lights and surveyed the tidy room that hadn't been used since Sam had moved the furniture down to the parlor for his client. He hadn't just dropped the sheets and blankets in a pile on the floor, as she'd expected. Since she didn't see them anywhere, she assumed he'd folded them and put them away.

Opening the double doors to Daphne's closet, Holly stood there, awestruck by the sight before her. It was the size of most bedrooms, lined with wooden built-ins that Sam had custom made for her enormous collection of clothing and shoes. Holly found what she was looking for on an upper shelf and cast around for some kind of step stool. She didn't find one, and she wasn't in the mood to hunt up a chair to stand on. Instead, she grabbed the edge of the plastic bag the linens were wrapped in, hoping to knock it down the lazy way.

Her approach worked well enough, but along with the bedding came an ornate Chinese box that popped open and spread its contents all over the plush carpet. Perfect. Already tired and grumpy, Holly nearly left the mess for later, until she noticed her name typed on a piece of heavy cream-colored parchment.

These papers were absolutely none of her business, she reminded herself sternly. Daphne had obviously hidden them away for a reason, and she had no right to intrude on her aunt's privacy. Then again, she'd have to pick them up to put them away, and it would be humanly impossible not to see what they contained. While she stood there debating with herself, a set of legal-sized documents caught her eye. At the top, in capital letters, she read a string of words that stopped her heart.

Pursuant to the Adoption of Holly Ann Mills.

Suddenly, she couldn't breathe.

Astounded to the point of dizziness, she sank down to the floor and put her head between her knees the way Dad had taught her when she used to get conked in the head playing junior league soccer. Emotions tumbled around inside her like a carnival ride, and she couldn't seem to get her balance.

With trembling hands, she picked up what she now understood was her original birth certificate, unlike the one that was sitting in a safe-deposit box in Boston. Even though she recognized how foolish she was being, she held it by the corner, as if that would somehow protect her from the truth. Her heart dreaded what it might say, but her mind had to know.

The very official document, filed in the State of California, listed Daphne as her mother, and someone named Ian Bennett as her father. She'd never heard him mentioned, even in whispers, but since her middle name echoed his, she didn't doubt the shocking revelation. It explained so many things that had always puzzled her about her family.

This was why her mother—loving and supportive as she was—had never understood Holly's flash-fire temperament. This was why she, the reasonably intelligent daughter of two career-minded college graduates, couldn't pay attention in class long enough to more than skate by but could happily sketch landscapes for hours.

Most important, this was why Daphne had always paid special attention to her. When she wasn't working in some exotic location, she'd entertained all three Fredericks girls on a regular basis, both in Savannah and her lavish home in Beverly Hills. But Holly was the one who'd spent more than one spring break with her in Paris. She was the one who'd had lunch with her favorite pop singer for her eighteenth birthday and got to frame her watercolors for display alongside Daphne's prized oils done by masters like Monet and Degas.

Holly wasn't the daughter of a social worker and a cop. She was the daughter of one of America's most beloved actresses and some mystery man. Everything she'd believed her entire life was a lie.

Once she'd recovered a bit, she carefully replaced the papers in their original order and nudged the exquisite box back into its cubbyhole. Moving on autopilot, she picked up the huge bagful of sheets and blankets and carried it downstairs. Mindful that she was still a little dazed, she grasped the unfinished handrail, carefully making her way down the steps and into her aunt's kitchen.

Her mother's kitchen, she amended with a frown.

Unable to process that at the moment, she went into the parlor to make the bed. While she worked, a picture of the entire family on Daphne's bedside table caught her eye. She had her own copy of it and had kept it beside her own bed since she was a child. Holly couldn't help noticing how much she resembled the woman she'd called Mom all these years. Then again, the Mills sisters looked so much alike, it was unlikely that anyone who didn't know them well had noticed anything out of the ordinary. The female family resemblance was so strong to the casual observer, the three younger girls were pretty much interchangeable.

Suddenly, instead of feeling paralyzed,

Holly was furious. How could all these people who supposedly loved her deceive her this way? Did they think she was so stupid that they could keep their dirty little secret from her forever?

Feeling very much alone, she was at a loss for what to do. She was tempted to call her lifelong friend Francine for a cathartic heart-to-heart, but nixed that when a horrifying notion flashed into her head.

What if Francine knew?

She was about the same age as Holly, and her mother, Valerie, and Daphne had been friends forever. Surely, they'd compared notes on their pregnancies, and when Daphne chose to give her baby away, Valerie would have known about it. Holly consoled herself with the knowledge that at least she hadn't been pawned off on strangers. Evidently, the Mills sisters had valued her enough to keep her in the family. Unfortunately, that train of thought led her to another, more sobering one.

Did her sisters know? They were younger than her, but not by much. By the time they came along, she was almost two, firmly established as the oldest child. But personality-wise, the younger two were like peas in a pod, and she'd always been the odd one out. They used to tease her about it, but they were both incredibly bright, and she couldn't imagine them not figuring it out at some point.

Even before that, her parents' friends and family must have noticed when the formerly un-pregnant Mrs. Fredericks showed up carrying a new baby. As her eyes filled with tears, Holly sank down on the plush mattress and stared at the picture she'd treasured for as long as she could remember.

Everyone knew, she concluded bitterly. Everyone but her.

Uncertain of what to do, she went into the kitchen to clean up the dinner dishes and give herself time to think.

Her mother.

Holly paused in the middle of drying a saucepan, rolling the phrase around in her head to see how it felt now that the initial shock had passed. She wasn't as livid as she'd been earlier on, but she couldn't decide if she was finally adjusting to the idea or had gone completely numb out of shock.

One thing was for sure, she decided as she dried the stack of pots and put them away, agonizing as it might be to yank everything out into the open, she couldn't tap dance around the truth for the next two months. At some point, they'd have to thrash through the past and figure out how it affected their future.

Because she couldn't hide out in the kitchen forever, she summoned her fleeting patience and headed into the den, where Chase and Daphne were watching the opening inning of a late baseball game. Well, Chase was watching, while Daphne flipped through a design magazine, dog-earing pages as she went.

When Holly came in, Daphne showed her a photo of an idyllic-looking patio scene. "I've always wanted something like this. What do you think of it?"

I think it would've been nice to know you're my mother.

Holly swallowed the bitter response, since technically she wasn't supposed to know she was Daphne's daughter in the first place. With that in mind, she kept things impersonal. "I think Sam would be able to build that with his eyes closed."

"Isn't he wonderful? I moved in just after Easter, and the weather was terrible. But there he was to welcome me to the neighborhood and help me get situated. So many people in town stared and pointed, but he treated me like an actual person. It was so nice."

Despite her gloomy mood, Holly couldn't help smiling at Daphne's glowing description of her neighbor. A girl could easily lose her head over a strong, capable guy like Sam

Calhoun. Not her, of course, she amended quickly. Her life had just gotten more complicated than ever, and now that she knew the deep, dark family secret, she had enough to manage without adding anything more into the mix.

Standing awkwardly in the middle of the room, she tried to come up with something to say. She'd never had that problem with Daphne before, but it was different now.

Everything was different now.

Leaning back into the throw pillows, Daphne ran a hand over Chase's head and went on, "I'm so glad you two were able to come. When you moved away from Savannah, I missed seeing you during my visits."

Holly wasn't touching that one—admitting any emotion at all would set her off. "We'll be here awhile. We'll have lots of time to catch up."

And maybe you can tell me what you were thinking when you decided to give me away, she added to herself grimly.

Before she blurted out something she couldn't take back, she said, "I need some air. Will you be okay for a little while?"

"Of course. Chase is teaching me about baseball, so take your time."

Forcing herself to walk normally instead

of bolting through the house, Holly opened the side door and quietly closed it behind her.

She couldn't leave Daphne and Chase completely alone, and even if she could, she had nowhere else to go. So she sank onto the porch steps and stared unseeing into the distance. Suddenly, the stark truth was more than she could bear, and as tears rolled down her cheeks, she buried her face in her hands and began to sob.

"Holly?" Sam plunked down on the step below her, and she angled her head just enough to see his worried face through her damp fingers. "What's wrong? Is Daphne okay?"

She'd forgotten he was still out here working, or she'd have gone to the front porch for some solitude. There was no help for that now, and she managed to choke out, "Just tired, is all."

"There must be more to it than that, to set you off like this. Wanna tell me?"

The sympathetic question only made her cry harder, and he slid up next to her. He put an arm around her, and in his mellow voice he said, "I know things seem bad right now, but they won't stay that way."

Something about his approach to the whole hysterical female thing was very comforting, and even in her current state, Holly recognized that it wasn't the first time he'd found a way to make her feel better. Sniffling, she looked up at him. "Promise?"

"Absolutely." Giving her an encouraging smile, he frowned when she started shivering. "It's pretty chilly out here for a Georgia peach like you. We should get you back inside."

"No." Shaking her head almost violently, she added, "I'm not ready yet."

Would she ever be ready to face her mother? she wondered. The way she felt right now, she honestly wasn't sure.

"Okay, but I can't let you sit out here freezing." Taking off his denim jacket, he draped it around her shoulders. That left him in nothing but a dusty T-shirt, but he didn't seem to notice. Rocking his worn boots back and forth on the step, he folded his hands and looked around. "Nights should be getting warmer soon."

She recognized his gallant attempt at making lame conversation, and out of gratitude she played along. "Really? How warm?"

"Sixties, sometimes seventies, depending on how the wind's blowing."

They chatted back and forth for a while, and the mindless chitchat did wonders for calming her nerves. While she was looking around the yard, she noticed the new garden retaining wall he'd been building was finished. He must have been on his way home when she derailed him with her meltdown.

Forcing confidence into her tone, she said, "I'm fine now. Thanks for stopping to check on me."

"You sure?" he asked with a doubtful look. "I know you're not supposed to say this to a lady, but you don't look fine to me."

He'd summed up her current state pretty well, but there was no point in him staying. Capable as he seemed, there was nothing he could do that would solve her problem. "You must have things to do at your place."

"Nothing that can't wait till tomorrow."

He was really sweet, this small-town boy with the hesitant grin and giving nature. If things had been different for her, it wouldn't take much for her to go head over heels for him.

"I appreciate that, but I should get back inside."

When she stood, he followed along in a gentlemanly gesture that seemed to be wired into his personality. Slipping off his jacket, she handed it to him. Tossing aside some of her caution, she held his gaze for a moment, searching for a reason not to trust him. She didn't find even a hint of one, and she decided to take a chance.

"Do you have any secrets, Sam?"

Those warning storm clouds blew through his eyes, and he nodded. "Everyone does."

"How do you handle yours?"

"One day at a time." Sympathy darkened his features, and he gave her a faint but determined smile. "Hang in there. It'll get better."

"Is that how it happened for you?"

"Not quite. I'm not where I wanna be, but I'm getting there."

The simple, honest confession stunned her. Especially because he'd so precisely summed up how she felt about herself right now. "I know what you mean. I guess I'm what you'd call a work in progress."

"Aren't we all?"

The dog tags he wore had found their way to the outside of his T-shirt, and he looked down as he toyed with the dull metal plates. She'd noticed him doing it many times, and suddenly she understood the reason behind it. "Those are Nate's, aren't they?"

Sam's head snapped up, and he pinned her with a sharp stare that made her regret speaking. The warm blue had vanished, replaced by a steely gray that sent a chill down her spine.

"Sam, I'm sorry." She backpedaled immediately. "It's none of my business, and I never should've brought it up."

"How could you possibly know they're not mine?" he demanded in a strangled whisper.

"I've met other veterans who wear someone else's tags in honor of a friend they lost," she answered as calmly as she could. The sorrow that clung to Sam had intensified to the point that she could almost feel it herself. Wanting to repay some of the kindness he'd shown her, she gently said, "Sometimes it helps to talk about what happened."

"Trust me—you don't wanna know."

She kept quiet while she waited for him to change his mind, but he remained stubbornly silent. She recognized the tactic from Brady's bag of tricks and knew that no matter how much she begged or coaxed, there was no way to convince Sam to confide in her if he wasn't ready.

Finally, she decided that she'd done all she could for tonight. "Okay, but if you ever change your mind, I'll be ready to listen anytime, day or night. All you have to do is start talking."

"There's things no one knows but me," he told her softly. "It's better that way."

Holly considered that in light of what she now knew about her own family and shook her head. "I'm not sure it is. Carrying around that kind of secret is hard on you, not to mention the ones who love you. The truth always comes out at some point, and it can really hurt the people you're trying to protect. Getting things out in the open might be hard, but in the end it's best for everyone involved. If Brady had been able to find a way to do that, he might still be alive."

Gazing at her intently, the former Ranger seemed to be absorbing what she'd told him. And then, to her amazement, the murkiness in his eyes shifted to reveal a hint of blue. "I appreciate you worrying about me, but I've got no intention of going that route."

"Too optimistic?"

"Too stubborn. I haven't got it all figured out yet, but I will."

Giving her a wry grin, he stood and headed down the steps and around the hedge to his own house. As she went back inside, she sent up a quick prayer for patience and courage. For both of them.

Too exhausted to do anything else, Holly

went into the den and fell into a comfy over-stuffed chair. "Where's Chase?"

"He's in his room reading that new wildlife book we bought for him when we were shopping."

"I'll go up and check on him in a few minutes. How are you feeling?"

Rolling her eyes, Daphne groaned melodramatically. "That physical therapist is an absolute sadist. I've never been so sore in my life. Not even the time that camel ran away with me in Egypt."

"It'll get easier," Holly said, hoping against hope that it was true. "I made a grocery run while Oliver was visiting this afternoon, so we're all stocked up again. What would you like for lunch tomorrow?"

"Lobster bisque and crab puffs."

"We don't have—"

"At The Minuteman," Daphne finished in a no-nonsense tone, referring to the town's iconic restaurant. "I haven't been there in weeks, and I want to see everyone. I'm way behind on the town gossip."

"I've got a fridge full of things to cook. What if I broil up some of that salmon I bought today? It's so fresh, I'm pretty sure it winked at me."

"No." Daphne pressed her lips together in

a firm line and shook her head like a petulant child. "I don't want people thinking I'm some helpless old lady, stuck in her house when summer's going on all around her. That's just pathetic."

She'd been out on various excursions several times, so she was hardly a prisoner, Holly groused silently. But she was too tired to be reasonable, so she shot back, "Why do you care what they think? You never have before."

"I do now."

As their argument spiraled into a full-on fight, Holly felt herself teetering on the edge of a meltdown. In her previous visits with Daphne, they'd spent their time jetting here and there or tooling around in her convertible, enjoying days filled with shopping and fun. While she considered herself to be competent and levelheaded, Holly was rapidly coming to the conclusion that she was totally unqualified as a chauffeur-slash-caregiver to the stars. Overwhelmed by frustration, she blurted out the question that had dominated her thoughts since she stumbled across the truth of who she was.

"Who's Ian Bennett?"

Chapter Eight

Every bit of color drained from Daphne's face, and she slumped back against the throw pillows in what Holly feared was an honest-to-goodness faint. Rushing forward, she caught her mother and was relieved to discover that she was still conscious.

But that was small consolation when she saw the horror that suddenly darkened the aging beauty's features. Holly had been the one to find Brady's lifeless body, and she had more experience with that kind of life-altering emotion than she'd prefer. She understood all too well how it felt to be blindsided that way.

"Where," Daphne asked in a strangled whisper, "did you hear that name?"

Holly had been prepared for anger or shock, but not anguish. Taking a moment to collect her thoughts, she sat on the coffee table and relayed how she'd found out who she really was. Then, a glimmer of hope flared and she asked, "Is it true?"

Daphne nodded, and that tiny spark winked out as if it had never existed. Those wide violet eyes gazed on her with a heart-wrenching mix of love and dread, but the exuberant woman she'd adored her entire life suddenly seemed very far away. They should have so much to say to one another, but neither of them seemed to be able to reach across the yawning chasm that had suddenly sprung up between them.

Love and patience were the only ways to bridge that kind of gap. Since she couldn't leave Daphne alone in her condition, Holly knew she'd be needing plenty of both to get through the rest of the summer in Liberty Creek.

They sat there for what felt like an eternity, and finally Daphne closed her eyes without saying anything more. Out of respect for her unspoken wishes, Holly retreated and left her to get some rest.

Since there was nothing more she could do until her mother was ready to talk, Holly spent some much-needed quiet time with Chase, hearing about his entertaining day at the mini golf course and letting him beat her at the well-used game of Chutes and Ladders she'd found at a yard sale.

At bedtime, they got on their knees beside his bed, and he began with the usual kid-related stuff before adding some more serious prayers.

"Take care of Dad," Chase said. After a pause, he went on, "And help Mom when she needs You, 'cause she won't ever ask."

Touched by the sentiment, she nudged his shoulder. "I save all my prayers for you."

He gazed up at her with those large, intelligent eyes that would forever remind her of the Brady she'd fallen in love with. "I know, but you should keep one for yourself. Everyone needs help sometimes."

"Where did you learn that?"

"Sam told me."

The former soldier had made it painfully clear that he was no longer the religious type, and she asked, "When?"

"When he came over the other day to bring Auntie and her wheelchair inside. I said it was nice of him to help us, and he said that's what neighbors do. I told him we didn't have that before, and he said it was a good thing we came here." Tilting his head with a quizzical look, Chase asked, "Do you think so, too?"

Considering what she'd so recently learned,

it was a toss-up, but Holly didn't want to upset him by expressing anything other than confidence about their current situation. Still, she didn't want to lie to him, either. So she settled on an explanation that she hoped would reassure him. "If I didn't, we wouldn't have done it. What do you think of Liberty Creek so far?"

"It's awesome," he replied without hesitation. "All the trees and this great big house for us to live in. Cody and my new friends are cool. And Sam," he added with a grin. "He's the best."

Chase didn't normally gush about adults this way, and Holly couldn't resist asking, "Really? What do you like so much about him?"

"Well, he likes the Red Sox. And when we were playing catch, he didn't throw easy balls for me like I was some little kid who couldn't catch a watermelon with a wheelbarrow."

Holly recognized the phrase as her father's and smiled until her new reality kicked in and reminded her that the colorful man was actually her uncle. This was going to take some getting used to, she thought glumly.

"Mom, is something wrong?"

"Not a bit, but you're stalling," she teased, standing to toss back his covers the way she did every night. "You're going to the new water park tomorrow with your summer rec crew, so you need a good night's sleep."

"Okay." Giving her a quick squeeze, he slid under the light blanket. "Night, Mom."

"Night."

Holly turned off the bedside lamp and retreated to the doorway. Looking back, she saw his peaceful face turned into the moonlight, eyes closed while he drifted off to dreamland. She didn't know how long she stood there, at once amazed by his resilience and humbled by the incredible responsibility of making sure that he made the most of the amazing potential he'd been born with.

Brady had failed their son, and Holly silently renewed her vow to never do the same.

She eased his door closed and slowly went downstairs, her feet dragging on every step. It had been a long, tiring day, and the last thing she wanted to do was confront the mother who'd inexplicably lied to her every day of her life.

Holly wished she'd kept the volatile secret to herself, at least until she came up with a way to address it in a logical manner. But the horse was out of the barn now, and there was no coaxing it back in. So she braced herself for some serious histrionics and joined Daphne in the cozy den.

Maybe she's asleep, Holly thought. That faint hope evaporated when those beautiful violet eyes swung to her as soon as she stepped into the parlor. Summoning the calmest tone she could manage under the circumstances, Holly asked, "Can I get you anything?"

"No, thank you."

An unspoken plea for understanding radiated from the expressive features that had earned Daphne Mills so many plum roles. *Incomparable*, more than one critic had dubbed her. If he'd added *incomprehensible*, Holly would have said he nailed it.

Uncertain of what to do, she sat in an armchair near the sofa and leaned back in a casual pose that she was pretty sure wasn't fooling either of them. Hunting for a way to start a conversation she'd never imagined having, she said, "So, I'm thinking you have a story to tell me."

Brow furrowed in confusion, Daphne shook her head. "I don't know where to start."

At the beginning? Holly nearly shot back, then remembered who she was talking to. Deceitful as she'd been, Daphne was still her mother, and Holly had been raised to be respectful. So she swallowed her bitterness and suggested, "How did you meet him?"

"I was shooting a movie in London," Daphne began, a slight smile softening the concern that had lined her face a few moments ago. "Ian Bennett was a Formula One driver, and the producer hired him to do some stunt work for the lead actor." She glanced over at the collection of frames on the mantel, nodding toward them. "That's him, in the center photo."

Holly slowly rose and went to take the picture from its spot. A tall, dark-haired man in a polo and khakis stood beside a sleek roadster, arms crossed as he grinned at the photographer, who must have been Daphne. Handsome didn't begin to describe him, and Holly wondered how many times she'd brushed past this photo, completely unaware that the young, carefree man was her father.

"Where is he now?" she asked, setting the frame back in place.

"In Heaven," her mother replied sadly. "We were engaged and planning our wedding when he was killed during a race. A few weeks later, I discovered I was pregnant. With you," she added with a trembling smile. "It was the saddest—and happiest—time of my life."

Some people might not have understood that, but Holly's own experience as a mother supporting a declining husband gave her a different perspective than she would have had otherwise. So, much as she wished she could remain indignant about the enormous lie, she felt her anger beginning to ebb slightly. "I can relate to that, I suppose. But that doesn't explain what happened after I was born. Was your career more important to you than I was?"

"Never," Daphne insisted vehemently, furious color rushing back into her cheeks. "More than anything, I wanted for us to be together. I even considered quitting the business, but then I realized that without my job, we'd have a terrible time of it. I didn't have any money put away, and since Ian and I weren't married, his life insurance money went to his parents. I needed to work to support us, and I thought I could balance the movies with caring for you."

"But?"

"Your mother—" Pausing, she amended, "My sister objected. She reminded me that the fishbowl of Hollywood is no place to raise a child. The adoption was her idea, to give you a normal childhood while still keeping me in your life. Eventually, I agreed with her, and when you were born, she and Don made you their daughter. It broke my heart whenever I had to leave after a visit with you. But I honestly believed it was the best situation for you."

Much as she hated to admit it, Holly saw the selfless logic in that. She'd do the same for Chase, putting aside her own feelings if she truly felt someone other than her was best for him. But that didn't cover everything. "Were you ever going to tell me the truth?"

"Every time I saw you," the aging star confided softly, tears welling in her eyes. "But we had so much fun together, and I didn't want to spoil that. The years slipped by, and then you married Brady and moved away, so I didn't see you as often. When I came to see Chase after he was born, it occurred to me that I was his grandmother." The misty look warmed with affection for her grandson. "I nearly told you then."

"But you didn't," Holly retorted, feeling the anger creeping in again. "Medical history is so important for a newborn. What if there was something I needed to know?"

"Gloria would've told you. She's his great-aunt, after all."

"She's not a doctor. What if she'd made the wrong call and it affected his health? Chase would've suffered for it."

Daphne blinked, pulling back in horror. "I never thought of that."

"From where I'm sitting, there's a lot of things you never thought of." She'd hoped that once they hashed everything out, she'd feel better. Unfortunately, it was turning out to be the opposite, and Holly felt the weight of it all crushing down on her. Pushing up from the arms of the chair, she said, "Well, I'm done for now. Let's get you into bed so we can both get some sleep."

Without argument, her patient complied, and in record time she was settled for the night.

"Do you need anything before I go upstairs?" Holly asked.

"No, thank you."

Holly headed for the door, then heard her name. Turning back, she braced herself for more tears. Instead, she saw contrition. "I'm so sorry for all the trouble this is causing you. I wanted you to grow up in the kind of warm, stable family I couldn't give you. But from the moment you were born, I loved you more than I ever thought possible. I hope one day you'll be able to forgive me."

"Me, too."

"If you want, I'll call a local service and have them send out a visiting nurse to help me until I'm on my feet again. That way, you and Chase can go back to Boston."

The irony of the situation was too much, and Holly didn't know whether to laugh or cry. Since crying didn't solve anything, she opted for a wry chuckle. "No, we can't. I had to get out of that depressing place, so I talked to the landlord a few days ago. He had a waiting list for our apartment, and he let me end the lease in June. Our stuff is in his storage area until I decide what to do. So, like it or not, we're here for the summer."

"You're welcome to stay as long as you need to. Would you be angry if I said I like it?"

"Maybe a little." Still, she couldn't help smiling at the generous offer. "But thank you for understanding. Chase doesn't get it, but I really think we need to start fresh in a new house and get on with the rest of our lives."

"Like me," her mother commented with a wry grin. "When I decided to retire, I wanted to get as far from LA as I could. Not just in miles, but in attitude. I discovered Liberty Creek during an antiquing trip, and as insane as it sounds, I just knew I was home."

"What about Savannah?"

"I was a girl there, and I loved it." Glancing around, she smiled proudly. "But this is my grown-up place. The one I chose for myself and can make my own."

"Is that why you picked something so run-down? Like a blank canvas for an artist?"

The woman she now knew as Mom tilted her head in a pensive gesture. "I suppose so. That hadn't occurred to me before, but it makes more sense than 'it spoke to me.'"

That prompted another thought, and Holly smiled. "Is that why you hired Sam as your contractor? Because he's a little run-down and needs some TLC?"

"That man has so much inside him but has no idea how to tap into it. You can see for yourself how talented he is, hardworking and loyal to boot. He served our country for years and needs some help getting back on his feet. Mostly, he needs someone to recognize his potential and give him a chance."

"I guess you're right about that," Holly admitted sadly. "If I'd found a way to make that happen for Brady, he might have been okay."

"No, Peaches," the older woman murmured with a frown. "When he came home, Brady was shattered beyond repair. You didn't cause his problems, so there was nothing more you could have done to solve them."

Because she was still reeling from their emotional heart-to-heart, the uncharacteristically philosophical statement caught Holly off guard. Strangely enough, no one had ever come right out and told her that Brady's deteriorating condition and eventual suicide weren't her fault. Then again, she'd never voiced the fear that she might somehow have been to blame, so she'd never given anyone the chance to reassure her.

Then again, Daphne was a consummate actress, famed for being able to conjure convincing emotions out of thin air. But those expressive eyes held nothing beyond sincerity, and Holly wondered if the flighty diva had more depth than anyone—including her own family—suspected.

Given the history lesson she'd received today, the concept wasn't as far-fetched now as it would have been before. Furious as she still was at the deceit, she couldn't deny that a part of her admired the woman who'd put aside her own wishes for the benefit of her child. Sadly, it reminded Holly of what she'd done for Chase, trying desperately to maintain some semblance of a family life even though she was the only one making the effort.

Maybe, she thought as she turned to go upstairs, she and her mother had more in common than she'd realized.

Drained from a long, challenging day, Holly

dragged herself up the steps and into her room. Out of habit, she left her door cracked in case Chase needed something in the middle of the night. She didn't bother changing, but collapsed into the grand four-poster bed in an exhausted heap. She closed her eyes, hoping to quickly fall asleep and leave her problems behind her for a few hours.

But it didn't work.

After some tossing and turning, she finally gave up and rolled onto her back to stare up at the ceiling. A shaft of moonlight was shining through the trees outside, and as the breeze wafted through the leafy branches, they made billowing shadows on the light-colored ceiling. She stared up at them for a while, letting the flowing images ease some of the aggravation she'd been fighting.

When she felt a light tap at the foot of the mattress, she glanced down to find a sleek black cat creeping toward her. Silvery whiskers twitching cautiously, her mother's enigmatic pet moved without a sound, placing each paw with care until she was sitting next to Holly. Cocking her head, Pandora blinked her enormous green eyes as if she was waiting for Holly to say something.

"Hello, there," she murmured gently to

avoid spooking the rarely seen cat. "It's nice to finally meet you."

Another blink, followed by a soft meow that sounded an awful like a question. She must be losing it, Holly thought, but when the sound was repeated, she decided it would be rude not to respond. "Yeah, it's been a tough day. Tomorrow will be better, though. Right?"

Pandora meowed again, but this time she followed it up by leaning down to rub cheeks with Holly and start purring. Holly had always been more of a dog person, but the sweet gesture was rapidly changing her opinion of cats being too standoffish to make good companions.

She reached out tentatively for a few gentle pats and kept going when the cat made it clear that she enjoyed the attention. To Holly's astonishment, the rhythmic motion actually made her feel better, so she kept doing it until they both fell asleep.

Chapter Nine

Another item off the punch list, Sam mused as he drew a line through *sand skim coat* with his flat-edged carpenter's pencil. He heard the family chatting out on the patio and stepped through the newly hung French doors to check in before he left.

"I buttoned everything up as much as I could to keep the dust down so you won't be choking on it. I'll start the primer tomorrow, and the paint should be done this weekend. The timing will be snug to finish everything, but I promise it'll be ready like you wanted."

"I was never worried about that," Daphne assured him. "But with all the extra time you're putting in, I wish you'd let me pay you as we go."

"Not a chance. We agreed on a timetable, and it's good enough for me." With that decided, he headed for his own place. "I'll be back in the morning, but if you ladies need anything before then, just call my cell."

"We will," Holly replied while she walked him through the yard to the gap in the hedge that had been widening from all the use it was getting. "Thanks again."

"Anytime."

The response leaped out on its own, and he was stunned to realize that he meant it. Normally, it took him a while to warm up to folks, but this bright, engaging woman had skirted around his usual defenses without even trying. She flashed him a grateful smile, and he got the same rustling feeling he had at the baseball meeting, a little stronger this time.

Fortunately for him, she turned and went back to the patio before he could make a complete fool of himself.

When he got to his front door, there was a jagged piece of notebook paper tacked to the frame.

Meet me at the forge. —Brian.

Groaning out loud, Sam tore the paper loose and took out his phone. It was the middle of the week, and for some crazy reason, Brian had made the fifty-mile drive to Liberty Creek. His shift started at 7:00 a.m., so that wasn't something he normally did.

Sam's radar was pinging loud and clear, and he hoped there wasn't something seriously wrong.

After calling up the number on his cell, he waited for his younger brother to answer. "What're you up to?"

"Nothin'," Brian replied smoothly, sounding like a kid trying to convince an adult that things were fine, when in truth the fire department was on their way.

"The forge has been closed for years," Sam pointed out curtly. "What kind of crazy idea have you come up with now?"

"Come down and find out for yourself. Or take a shower and go to bed early. Your call."

The final two words simmered with a challenge, and even though Sam was just about dead on his feet, his curiosity got the better of him. "Ten minutes, Brian. That's all you're getting from me."

"That's all I need, big brother. See ya soon."

Sighing to himself, Sam dragged his feet back out to his work truck and drove through the village to the wide-open spot that had been the perfect location for a blacksmithing operation. Close enough to the bridge and town to be accessible but far enough out that the coal fires wouldn't choke the residents. There he found Brian's four-by-four parked outside the long-shuttered business that had given generations of local families their livelihoods. The day Granddad locked the doors had been one of the darkest for the Calhouns.

A week later, he died in his sleep. Much as Sam hated superstition, to this day part of him still believed that closing down his beloved tinkering spot had broken his grandfather's heart, and it simply stopped.

Batting the gloomy thought aside, Sam climbed out of the cab and met his brother on the cracked sidewalk in front of the faded sign.

Liberty Creek Forge, est. 1820

Because this wasn't his idea, Sam folded his arms and waited for Brian to start.

"Thanks for coming," he began, looking slightly less sure of himself now that Sam was actually here. "I know you're real busy."

The humble tone in his voice was very un-Brian-like, and Sam allowed his stern expression to soften a little. "It sounded important, and my leftovers aren't going anywhere. What's up?"

Brian grimaced, then let out a heavy sigh. "I got laid off today." When Sam didn't respond, Brian let out a bitter laugh. "Yeah, I know, again. No matter how good you are, everyone thinks they can get by with one less machinist on the shop floor. And when you're the low man on the totem pole, you're the one who gets the ax."

"Then you get a new job 'cause you're good at what you do, but you're the low man again," Sam added sympathetically. "I get it, and I'm sorry you're having such a bad run. But what brings you here?"

"I'm tired of getting fired because management can't figure out how to balance the books any other way," Brian said bluntly. "I wanna be the boss."

He motioned to the locked sliding doors, and Sam frowned. "Of what? This place was a dinosaur when you were born. What makes you think it's gonna be any different all these years later?"

"Folks love one-of-a-kind things. We take that kind of stuff for granted because we grew up with it, but a lot of people are sick of having the same furniture and decorations their neighbors do. They shop at the same places, so every yard and patio looks like the next."

"Okay, but what has that got to do with you?"

"I can make anything out of metal." The statement was pretty much accurate, but Sam couldn't help chuckling, which made Brian scowl defensively. "You know it's true."

"Yeah, it is. I'm just yanking your chain."

Brian tilted his head with a curious look. "You haven't done that since you came home. Something happen recently?"

Nothing he could define, Sam thought, shaking his head. "Not really. Go ahead."

"Anyway, I was stomping around my place, looking for something to throw. I grabbed one of those iron candlesticks I made with Granddad here in his hobby shop when I was a kid. It was heavy, and while I stood there holding it, I had a brainstorm. Reopen the ironworks and use the old forge to make things for customers who want unique pieces for decorating. The story of how it's made by hand in America would be a bonus and give us an edge over the assembly-line approach."

"Like at that Renaissance festival they have every summer outside Waterford," Sam commented in a pensive tone. "Folks love watching that blacksmith work, and he gets a small fortune for the bigger things he makes."

"Yeah, but I'm not wearing tights for anyone," Brian commented with a sour look. "Plus, once we get up and running, we could advertise the place for the tourists who visit the area every year. There's always lots of them around for the fall colors, and we could have at least a small work space ready by then, maybe take some orders that could be ready to ship a couple weeks later."

He'd obviously been thinking about this for a while, and the sting of his most recent job loss had fanned the spark into a flame. Then it occurred to Sam that the verbiage had gradually shifted from "I" to "we," and he chuckled. "When you say 'we,' I'm guessing you mean you and me."

"And Jordan," Brian added, eyes lighting with enthusiasm at the mention of their favorite cousin. "I don't wanna get his hopes up, but I'm sure he'd be interested in at least talking about it. Traveling around with those art shows is fun, but the last time he was here, he told me that the feast-or-famine income thing is getting old. He's looking to settle down, and I figure here is as good as anywhere."

Sam wasn't at all certain that Jordan would agree on that, but he didn't want to dampen Brian's excitement, so he kept his doubts to himself. Instead, he grabbed the heavy chain and padlock and gave it a good yank. It was solid Calhoun workmanship and didn't even creak. "Have you got a key?"

"Right here." Leaning down, Brian picked up a heavy-duty set of bolt cutters. He set them in place and each brother took one of the long handles, pushing them together until the bar on the old lock gave way with a resounding snap.

Crazy as it seemed, Sam couldn't help thinking that it was as if the old building knew what was happening and was voicing its approval of Brian's idea to bring it back to life.

Brian slipped the chain loose and coiled it before dropping it on the ground. Grinning at Sam, he took hold of one iron handle and waited for Sam to grab the other. The mechanism was seized with rust, so their first tug got them precisely nowhere. After a few more pulls, the corroded wheels began to loosen and moved along the upper track with a drawn-out screech that made a nearby dog howl in protest.

"I know how he feels," Sam grunted, putting his back into the job.

Finally, they opened the doors far enough for Brian to sweep a flashlight around the interior. The scuttling of tiny feet and sound of flapping wings told them the place wasn't completely deserted, and when a bat soared over his head to escape, Sam chuckled. "I'm thinking the first thing you need is an exterminator. A brave one."

Brian laughed and boldly stepped through the opening. "Come on. Let's see what we've got to work with."

"I didn't say yes yet," Sam pointed out, but followed after him, anyway. He'd served ten years in the Army, after all. A few flying rodents were nothing.

The electricity was still off, so they could only see what was illuminated by the beam of Brian's light. Hulking in the darkness were piles of steel that seemed to be waiting for someone to feed them into the forge. Tarps that had been thrown over the raw material were covered in dust and bird droppings, and the air was thick with the scents of mildew and rot.

This had been his family's business since just after the Revolution, Sam thought morosely. Seeing it left for dead like this was depressing, to say the least.

"For once, I'm glad Granddad isn't here," Brian said quietly. "He loved this old place, and seeing it like this would've killed him."

Out of respect for their grandfather, they were silent for several moments. Then Brian turned to Sam with a hopeful look. "I know it's a disaster, and there's no guarantee this will even work. But there's no way I can do it on my own, and I can't afford to pay anyone for a while. Will you help me get the forge back on its feet? For Granddad?"

This venture was as near to a hopeless

cause as Sam could imagine, but for his brother's sake, he dredged up a grin. "Yeah, I'm in. Whattya need?"

Holly had just left the dry cleaners when her phone began singing Daphne's signature ringtone. Oliver had generously offered to stay with her while Holly ran errands, so she'd planned on having at least an hour before she had to pick up Chase. Anticipating an emergency, Holly's heart shot into her throat, and she swallowed hard before answering. "Hello?"

"Hi, Peaches!" Daphne hollered, a rush of wind in the background nearly drowning out her voice. "Can you hear me all right?"

"Yes, but where are you? In a wind tunnel?"

"Out with Oliver in his beautiful new car. His mechanic just finished restoring it, so we're seeing what it can do."

"You're supposed to be at home resting," Holly seethed. Elegant gentleman or no, she was going to throttle Oliver Chesterton next time she saw him.

There was a muffling sound, as if Daphne had covered the microphone for a sidebar conversation. Then she heard the scoundrel's voice. "Don't let her worry you, Holly. Daphne is properly cushioned and strapped in, and this car is older than I am, so I'm staying well below the speed limit. You have my word on that."

"You are absolutely no fun," Daphne huffed in the background, but Oliver simply chuckled.

Despite the scare they'd given her, Holly couldn't help but smile. Accustomed to a jet-setting lifestyle and plenty of pampering, Daphne's forced inactivity had left her aching for some excitement. At least she and Chase were having fun this summer, she groused silently, trying not to be envious of their spontaneity. By necessity, everything she did was planned to the nth degree, and she was human enough to admit that there were times she wished she could go off-script and enjoy herself for a change. But she couldn't, so she did her best to be happy for her mother. "So, Bonnie and Clyde, what are your plans?"

Oliver repeated the notorious reference and chuckled. "We're driving to Briarton to see a traveling theater troupe that's doing Shakespeare in the Park. Then it's off to dinner at The Walden, my friend's new restaurant. I have Daphne's wheelchair and medication, and you have my word that she'll be using both as prescribed by her doctor."

"Sounds fabulous. You two kids have fun."

They sang a jubilant goodbye to her, and she shut down her phone before putting it in her bag. The tiny business district of Liberty Creek stretched for about a city block, so she could see most of the town from where she stood.

Two mountain bikes turned the corner, their custom license plates tagging them as rentals. They passed by her, and she caught the scent of something scrumptious wafting out the open front door of Ellie's Bakery and Bike Rentals. She wandered in that direction, suddenly hungry for a treat.

Behind the counter, she found the always-smiling owner. "Something smells amazing in here."

"Just a few treats I'm whipping up for the crew over at the forge today. I want to make sure my boys get a good lunch while they're working so hard."

It was cute how she referred to the Calhoun brothers, as if they were children she was proud of instead of full-grown men. Then again, Holly would probably feel the same about Chase when he was older, too. "Sam hasn't said much, other than that he got shanghaied into helping. How's it going?"

"I'm not sure myself," Ellie admitted with

a laugh. "I take that to mean they're still in the cleaning-out phase."

"I'd really like to contribute somehow. How about if I deliver these, along with some desserts? Cookies and cupcakes usually work best for a picnic spread."

"Now you've got the idea. Help yourself to whatever you'd like while I pull a couple boxes of treats together."

Holly felt like a little girl after school, enjoying a snack while her mother got dinner started. Then she remembered that it had been her aunt chopping vegetables and seasoning meat with her secret-recipe concoctions of herbs and spices. Suddenly, the melt-in-your-mouth slice of pound cake tasted like sawdust, and she swallowed hard around the lump clogging her throat.

Before she knew what was happening, tears were rushing down her cheeks, even as she struggled to keep them in check. Holly found herself wrapped in a pair of motherly arms, being rocked like a child who'd fallen and was in need of comforting.

"There, there, now," Ellie crooned in a soft tone that spoke of plenty of practice making people feel better. "Nothing's ever so wrong that it can't be made right."

Holly didn't trust herself to talk right now,

but she forced herself to take a deep breath and nod.

Ellie pulled a couple of napkins from the dispenser and handed them to her. "Do you want to tell me about it?"

"No, I'm fine," Holly insisted, desperately trying to pull herself together. "Just tired, is all."

Ellie clucked in sympathy. "Of course you are. So much to do, running that crazy household all by yourself, and the baseball project besides. It's a lot for one person to handle."

She'd nailed the way Holly had been feeling but had been unwilling to share. She didn't want anyone to think that she was anything other than completely capable, when in truth she often felt as if she wasn't up to the tasks that she'd set for herself. That someone who barely knew her had diagnosed her problem suggested that it wasn't all that uncommon, and it dawned on her that she might be able to learn something from Sam's compassionate grandmother. "Some days, I feel like nothing I do is good enough."

"We all do," Ellie assured her confidently. "And then there are days when we get things just right, and we wonder if anyone notices."

"Exactly."

"Someone always notices, though," she

said, nodding at the cross Holly wore, "and His strength keeps us going whether we realize it or not."

Holly fingered the silver symbol of her faith, recalling the day Daphne gave it to her before they attended church with the family. It had been Holly's first exposure to the faith she held so close, in good times and bad. Now that she knew the truth of their relationship, she wondered if her mother had been trying to give her something tangible that would always connect them.

Feeling calmer now, she took a deep breath and forced a smile. "You're absolutely right. Thanks for reminding me."

"You're very welcome. Now, let's get these things packed up for the boys. They should be ready for a break by now."

Nodding, Holly gulped down the rest of her anxiety and filled large to-go cups with lemonade and iced tea. Long ago, she'd learned that the best way to forget your troubles was to do something thoughtful for someone else. It made everyone feel better, and your own troubles faded into the background. At least for a little while.

Draping the carryout bags over her wrists, she carefully balanced the drink trays and made her way down the street. The huge doors to the ironworks were latched, but she could hear plenty of commotion on the other side. She waited for a reasonable lull and hollered, "Break time!"

At first, she thought no one had heard her, but then she heard footsteps approaching and someone releasing the lock before sliding the door partway open.

She'd only seen Brian from a distance, and he was much dustier than he'd been at church. But she recognized him as he flashed her what she could only describe as a wolfish grin. "Hello, there, gorgeous. What can I do for you?"

"I'm Holly Andrews," she explained politely. "Daphne Mills's niece." *Sort of,* she added silently.

"Oh, I've heard all about you," he filled in with another grin. This one was slightly less predatory, but not by much. Offering a hand, he said, "Brian Calhoun. Did my grandmother send you?" he added, nodding at the bakery boxes she held.

"Sort of. I was coming by to check on your progress and offered to bring these with me."

"Then follow me."

He turned away, and she glanced around, hoping Sam might be somewhere nearby and come to her rescue. But she saw no sign of the towering contractor, so she followed Brian to a makeshift table made of some planks laid across two sawhorses. The stainless steel commercial coffee maker it held looked decidedly out of place in its rustic surroundings, but she set her goodies down beside it.

"Whattya think of our snack shop?"

"Interesting."

He gave her a knowing look as he poured steaming coffee into a beat-up mug with the logo of an anvil and Liberty Creek Forge stenciled on it. Handing it to her, he commented, "That's the tone women use when they don't have the heart to tell you you're boring them to death."

"Got me there." Saluting him with her drink, she took a delicious swallow and sighed. "That's really good."

"Everyone has hidden talents," he said.

"Leave the lady alone," Sam growled, punctuating the order with the head of a greasy wrench. "If Daphne finds out you've been pestering her niece, she'll make sure you regret it."

"I'm not pestering," Brian assured him easily, sweeping Holly with a very male glance. "I'm admiring."

"Drooling, more like it. If you want the electricity in the office working before the next century, you'd best go get me a spare fuse. The old one's shot."

"In case you forgot, this is my place," the younger brother retorted, tapping his chest for emphasis. "You get it."

In response, Sam folded those impressive arms across his broad chest, glaring down at the forge's new owner. He didn't say a word, but apparently he didn't have to. Heaving a long sigh, Brian slunk toward the open door that led to the cellar and trudged down the stairs like a pouting child who'd just been sent to his room.

Shaking his head, Sam turned back to her with a mischievous gleam in his eyes. At first, she didn't understand the significance, but she quickly caught on. "Those parts aren't down there, are they?"

In answer, he pulled something from the front pocket of his jeans and held up what must have been the piece he needed.

"So you sent him off to what? Preserve my honor?"

"Little brothers. Can't live with 'em, can't throw 'em off the roof. Since you're out and about, I'm assuming Daphne is, too."

"Oliver took her over to Briarton for the Shakespeare in the Park festival, and then dinner at someplace called The Walden," Holly explained, doing her best not to feel jealous.

"I've heard about that restaurant. It's always booked solid, so you've gotta know the owner to get a reservation sometime this year."

"Or be a famous movie star."

"I guess that'd work, too."

When he noticed Brian had returned, Sam angled a mock glare at him. At least, she hoped he was kidding because that look could kill. "What?"

"There are no fuses downstairs," Brian retorted in an accusing tone. "If I didn't know better, I'd think you were trying to get rid of the competition."

"In your dreams, little brother," Sam growled back.

"While you're goofing around, I'll just take this into the back," Brian snarled as he shouldered a case marked Cast Iron Fittings and headed for the storeroom. "Nice to meet you, Holly."

Sam glowered at him, but it didn't have much effect since he was walking away and couldn't see it. When he turned back to her, Holly asked, "Are you two always like this?"

"Pretty much. Says he's making up for when I was gone and there was no one else around here worth fighting with."

"That's his way of saying he missed you. My sisters and I are pretty much the same way."

Except they were her cousins, she amended silently. That was really going to take some getting used to.

"Something wrong?"

Startled by the question, Holly angled a look at him. "Why?"

"That's just about the biggest sigh I ever heard. Are you worried about Daphne being out of the house for so long? Because I can promise you, Oliver treats her like she's made of glass. If there's any sign of trouble, he'll drive her straight to the nearest hospital, no matter what she says."

Comforted by his confidence in the dapper gentleman, Holly relayed the gist of their open-air conversation, and Sam grinned. "That sounds like them. They're quite the item around town."

"Daphne's an item no matter where she goes." A disturbing possibility occurred to her, and she chose her next words very carefully. "Do you know how they met?"

"At the Harvest Festival last fall when she was here on vacation with some friends," he replied with a shrug. "Why?"

"I don't know how to ask this politely, so please don't take it the wrong way."

"Okay."

"I know she comes across as being so-phisticated, but when it comes to men, she doesn't always have the best judgment. She's had some bad experiences in the past with men thinking, well, that they'd like to get their hands on her money." Sam burst out laughing, and Holly glared at him. "What's so funny?"

"Don't tell me you don't recognize Oliver's last name."

She rolled it around in her mind for a mo-ment until something clicked. Her jaw fell open in astonishment, and when she'd recov-ered a bit, she asked, "You mean, he's one of *those* Chestertons? The Chestertons that own half the property in New England?"

"Yes, ma'am. He's got more money than any ten people could ever spend. Even your aunt."

"Wow. Well…I…" Recognizing that she'd started to stammer, Holly paused to get her brain back in proper working order. Seeing the humor in the situation, she finally laughed. "I'm glad I asked you about this and not him. That would've been embarrassing."

"My guess is he would've answered your question and told you he's got nothing but good intentions where Daphne's concerned. Probably would've admired you for looking out for her that way, too."

"She's family," Holly said reflexively, more than a little surprised to hear herself say that considering the awful time she'd been having accepting the Mills sisters' well-guarded secret.

"Yeah, she is," he agreed with one of those wry grins. "That's how I got roped into working down here with Brian today."

Glancing around, she shook her head. "This place looks like it's been empty for a long time. Do you really think he can get a viable business going here?"

"A month ago, I'd have figured it'd be as likely as us having four junior baseball fields ready for games in mid-July. But seeing as that's gonna be happening, I guess anything's possible."

"That's how it works when you get a bunch of dedicated sports parents all pulling in the same direction."

"Not to mention Daphne's generous donation to the cause. That was really nice of her."

"That's my mother," Holly commented with genuine affection. "When it comes to kids, her checkbook's always open."

Sam didn't say anything, just stared at her

in obvious confusion. She couldn't imagine why, but when she replayed the last bit of their conversation over in her head, she identified her slip. Maybe he would assume she'd just misspoken, she thought hopefully. So, as she'd done whenever she messed up during her childhood dance recitals, she decided that the best thing she could do was keep on going.

"So," she said briskly, purposefully looking around to avoid his curious gaze, "what can I do to help?"

"Oh, no, you don't," Sam muttered, taking her elbow to guide her to a relatively quiet corner away from the crew of friends Brian had assembled to help him. When they were standing in reasonable privacy, Sam folded his arms in a pose that clearly said he wasn't moving until she explained herself. "Was this what you were so upset about the other night when you asked me about having secrets?"

That he recalled the exact time of her meltdown touched her in a completely unexpected way. With everything else that had gone on since then, their very honest discussion had faded from her memory. But apparently not for Sam. A quick look around showed her that no one was paying any attention to them, so in a hushed voice, she related what she'd found in her mother's closet.

"I remember that box," he commented pensively. "I'd never seen anything like it, and she told me it was made by an artisan she knew in Italy. I said there must be something special inside, and she gave me kind of a sad smile. She said that to her, the contents were priceless."

The overwhelming emotions Holly had experienced in the bakery earlier bubbled to the surface, and a look of panic seized Sam's face. "That was stupid of me, Holly. I'm so sorry."

"No, it's—" taking a deep breath, she steadied her voice "—sweet."

"She really loves you. And she's crazy about Chase. I guess now it makes sense why she talks about you two all the time. I mean, she's got dozens of friends all over the world, but you're the people she talks about most."

As Holly absorbed what he'd told her, the knot in her throat began to loosen. Maybe it was because she'd already come to grips with the truth and just didn't recognize it. Or maybe she trusted that Sam would never lie to her and she believed him.

Whatever the reason, she left the forge that day feeling lighter than she had in a long time. And it was wonderful.

Chapter Ten

When you grew up in a place called Liberty Creek, the Fourth of July was a pretty big deal.

Sam had skipped the festivities last year, but somehow he'd gotten roped into pulling a float in this morning's parade. Basically, he recalled with a grin, Chase had asked him, and he'd agreed. Holly was right—the kid was impossible to refuse.

"How's that?" the kid in question asked, stepping back to check over the bunting they were stringing on the walls surrounding the bed of Nate's dark blue pickup. It sat in Daphne's driveway, freshly cleaned and waxed for its star turn in this morning's parade.

Sam was going over the towing lines, and he glanced up to see how the decorating was going. "Looks good. Do the same on the other side, and I think the baseball moms will be happy."

"Can I ride up front?" the boy asked eagerly.

"I thought you were sitting on the float with Cody and your other teammates."

"I'd rather be with you."

The honest sentiment hit Sam in a way he never could have predicted. Pleased beyond words, he made a show of thinking it over before nodding. "As long as your mom's okay with it, I could use a copilot. Don't wanna run over any of the Girl Scouts."

Chase laughed. "You'd never do that, anyway. But thanks."

"Anytime, sport."

"That's what Cody's dad calls him," Chase commented as he circled around the cab to the other side of the truck. "I like it."

Between his years away in the service and his recent struggles, Sam had never considered himself to be father material. He loved and respected his own father and had often wished he could follow in his footsteps. Because of that, being compared to another dad was a new experience for Sam. While he rolled the concept around in his mind, he was shocked to discover that it didn't feel as awkward as he'd expected it to. Maybe his faint hope of having a family someday wasn't as unfounded as it had once seemed.

"That looks great, guys," Holly said as she came over to join them. Coming forward, she rattled the contents of a large plastic tub. "These are the favors the committee and I have been putting together for the last couple days. They're nets of candy with a tag about joining up for baseball. Practices start next week, and we're hoping this will bring in more kids."

"Those are awesome, Mom! Can I have some to toss out of the truck while we're in the parade?"

Holly gave Sam a quizzical look, and he explained what Chase was referring to. "Only if it's all right with you, though. He was supposed to ask first," he added, sending a mock glare toward his wannabe wingman.

After a moment, she said, "If that's what he wants, then it's fine with me. Are you sure he won't be a distraction for you?"

"Probably, but I can manage. Was Daphne excited to get out for the town's Independence Celebration?"

Holly laughed. "Worse than Chase. She was ready an hour before Oliver came to get her. Her physical therapist said she'll probably only need the wheelchair for a few more weeks, so soon it will be easier for her to go out the way she used to. She's always been a people person, and she really misses seeing everyone."

Sam was thrilled to hear that his generous neighbor was doing so well. But in the back of his mind, he knew that once Daphne was able to get around on her own again, Holly and Chase would be heading back to Boston. The idea of them leaving threatened to derail his bright mood, and he forced himself to focus on just enjoying today.

Chase's voice brought him back to earth. "Sam, do you have anything to put some candy bags into?"

Reaching over the seat, he pulled out a box that had once held a pair of Nate's work boots. For once, his decision to leave the truck just as it was made a little sense. "How's this?"

"That'll work."

The response was something Sam often said, and it occurred to him that it wasn't the only saying of his that the boy had adopted since they'd gotten to know each other. It was flattering to be admired that way, he realized. Knowing that Chase thought enough of him to copy him made him feel more optimistic about...well, pretty much everything.

The three of them sang along with the radio

during the drive into town. Main Street had been closed down for the town-wide celebration, and Sam pulled into the large vacant area near the forge where the parade participants were gathering to get organized. Seeing people milling around here again was encouraging, and for Brian's sake, he hoped that all this activity was a sign of more positive things on the way.

Sam maneuvered the truck around to park in front of a flatbed wagon that had been outfitted with rails and a decent approximation of a baseball diamond. Somehow, the T-shirts Holly had rush-ordered for the league had arrived in time, and the players were decked out in the different colors their coaches had chosen for each team.

"The kids look happy," he commented as they left the truck. "You and the other team parents did a great job."

"It was touch and go for a while, but I only had to threaten the print shop twice."

The stern edge on her tone was very much at odds with her sweet appearance, and he chuckled. Anyone foolish enough to underestimate this feisty single mom was in for a rude shock if they tested her patience. "Good thing for them, huh?"

"Very." Chase was sitting on the ledge of

the open passenger window, and she pointed at him. "Behave yourself, and have fun. I'll see you in the square after the parade."

"We'll be there. At church on Sunday, Emma told me she's bringing the apple pie that won her a prize in the county fair last year. She promised me the first piece."

From his higher vantage point, he swiveled to watch the fire trucks rolling into position, and she smiled up at Sam. "I can't thank you and your family enough for making us feel so welcome here. It hasn't been easy, but you've all made it a lot better than it could have been."

Her gratitude struck a chord with him, telling him how lonely her existence had been in Boston. "Just being neighborly. That's how we do things here."

Her smile deepened, taking on a warmth that hadn't been there before. "I know. That's one of the things I like most."

Sam got the distinct impression that she was trying to tell him something without coming right out and saying it. It wasn't like him to read into things that way, but he asked, "About the town? Or me?"

"Both."

Something he couldn't quite define sparkled in her eyes before she turned away and climbed aboard the float. More than a little stunned by her revelation, he absently handed up the tote of goodies and found himself staring up at her. Sam had no clue how long he stood there, eyes locked with hers, knowing he should move but seemingly incapable of making it happen. Fortunately for him, someone set off an air horn to alert everyone that it was time to get lined up for the parade.

Sam hitched the wagon to his truck, triple-checking the connections to make sure they were securely attached. Then he got into the cab and waved that everything was set.

Glancing over at his shotgun rider, he grinned. "Ready?"

"Yup." In emphasis, Chase rattled the box of netting-wrapped candy.

"You've got a strong arm, so make sure you take it easy with those," Sam cautioned as he slowly pulled the float into place. "You don't wanna hurt anyone."

"Okay." Familiar laughter filtered through the open back window, and Chase looked back. "Mom really likes the baseball parents. It's nice that she's having fun."

"Yeah, it is."

"In Boston, she was sad a lot of the time," the boy continued in a voice that was far too serious for someone his age. "She tried to be happy, but I could tell she wasn't."

Sam couldn't imagine how tough it had been for them, and he searched for some encouraging words. "Things are better now, though, so that's good."

"I really like it here," Chase informed him, smiling as the marching band in front of them began the opening tune of a patriotic medley. "It's easy to make friends when people are so awesome."

His observation echoed what his mother had said earlier, and knowing that he'd had a small part in that made Sam feel prouder than he had in a long time. "I'd imagine so."

For the rest of their ride, Chase alternated between launching treats out into the crowd and regaling Sam with a long list of his favorite things about Liberty Creek. Sam was pleased to hear that he was near the top, right after Daphne, of course. After a quick breath, the boy went on to say he also prized the bakery that stocked his preferred snacks, Hal's collection of vintage video games and the quaint church where he attended Sunday school.

It occurred to him that Chase was impressed by things Sam had taken for granted most of his life. Hearing about them from a kid's perspective gave him a new appreciation for his hometown and all it had to offer.

And for the first time in longer than he cared to recall, he felt grateful just to be here.

The parade slowly made its way down Main Street, pausing here and there when one group or another needed some extra time. The stalls gave him a chance to take in the red, white and blue decorations that had gone up around town in the past few days. And it wasn't just the business district that was decked out, he noticed. Every house was flying an American flag, and there was enough bunting draped over porch railings and fences to make even the Founding Fathers proud.

The band led everyone to the war memorial that stood in a quiet corner of the square behind the old-fashioned gazebo that was adored by everyone from tourists to local wedding couples. Careful to stay clear of the people strolling in, Sam pulled alongside the fire trucks and stepped out to help his passengers down from their float.

"We're a hit," Holly told him excitedly, giving Chase an exuberant hug. "A bunch of people waved their favors at us and promised to sign up. If even half of them carry through on it, we'll be in great shape."

"We'd better get that last backstop installed,

then," Sam replied with a chuckle. "Sounds like we'll be needing it."

"Definitely." She smiled over at Chase. "So, this is a little different from how Boston does things for the Fourth. What do you think of it?"

"It's better," he replied without hesitation. "I never got to be in the parade before."

"Good point."

They drifted along with the crowd heading for the memorial, where a middle-aged man in formal Army attire was waiting for everyone to arrive. Sam noted that he bore the insignia of a chaplain, and out of habit he braced himself for the onslaught of emotions he'd come to expect whenever he was confronted with a remnant of his military past.

But it never materialized.

Not even several minutes later, when the preacher asked them all to bow their heads while he prayed for the safe return of soldiers stationed around the world. Out of the corner of his eye, Sam saw Holly glance over at him, as if she was concerned about his reaction to the religious ceremony.

It felt good to be able to give her a muted smile to let her know he was fine. It felt even better when her hand discreetly reached out to give his a little squeeze of approval, lingering there until a small choir finished singing the national anthem.

"And now," the pastor solemnly announced, "while this is a day of rejoicing, it hasn't come without a cost. I'd like us to take a moment to recognize those who have fallen in defense of the liberties that we often forget to be thankful for."

Standing at the edge of the small park, a lone trumpeter began playing "Taps," and Sam's confidence started to falter. When a trumpet off in the distance picked up the melancholy tune, in his memory he flashed back to military funerals he'd attended while he was in the service. Then his imagination took over, giving him the morose impression that the two instruments represented Nate and him, one forever out of reach, the other hopelessly lost without him.

Head still bowed, Sam held a hand over Nate's dog tags, wishing for something that could never be. He didn't register Holly's fingers wrapping around his until he felt his own grasping them in a desperate attempt to ground himself in reality. Apparently, Chase sensed that something was wrong, and the sensitive boy stepped closer to Sam in a protective gesture that touched him deeply.

Bracketed by two of the bravest people he'd

ever met, he made it through the short but emotionally charged service that not long ago would have driven him off in a rage. And, for the first time since coming home, Sam believed that in spite of all the wrong turns he'd taken along the way, he was finally where he belonged.

What a fabulous group of people.

Holly was painting one of the long wooden benches that had been donated by the school, and she paused to marvel at the progress that had been made at the baseball complex in just a few short weeks. Unless you'd seen the overgrown property before its transformation, you'd never guess that it had been a de facto wildlife sanctuary and not four perfectly groomed diamonds for kids to use.

Over on the field that was being prepped for the girls' softball teams, she saw Hal Rogers and his granddaughter raking out the broad swath of dirt that made up the large infield. Lynette had a softball with her, and she stepped into the pitching circle, yelling for Cody to stand in as her catcher. After some warm-up stretches, she whipped her arm around in the windmilling underhand motion unique to the sport and delivered a perfect strike. Shouting his approval, Cody gave her a thumbs-up before tossing the ball back.

Even in Boston, Holly had seldom seen a field dedicated to junior softball. If more people knew about this one, she mused, they might attract even more girls from the area to join the Liberty Creek teams. More registration fees, more concession revenue—it could only be a positive for the long-term outlook of the league.

"Uh-oh," Sam said as he strolled over with a bottle of water that he handed to her. "I know that look. You're redesigning something in your head, aren't you?"

Holly laughed at his description, then took a long swallow of the water she hadn't been missing until now. Sam seemed to have a knack for guessing what she needed even before she knew it herself. In her experience, that was an unusual quality for a man, and it was one she definitely appreciated.

When she shared her sports mom epiphany, he immediately nodded. "It's a great idea, and I'd imagine everyone would jump on board that wagon. You should bring it up at the boosters meeting at the beginning of August."

Her last boosters meeting, she added silently, a little saddened by the realization. She'd come to Liberty Creek knowing that their stay would be over when Daphne was fully back on her feet. According to the team of doctors caring for her, three more weeks would do the job, and she'd be her old self again.

Then Holly and Chase would be heading back to Boston and whatever came next for them. She should start hunting for apartments online, she supposed. The trouble was, whenever she opened her computer to browse the rental listings, she quickly lost interest and switched to a topic she was more enthused about. Custom jerseys, discounted kids' cleats, kittens batting at dogs' wagging tails. Anything, really, other than what she was supposed to be doing.

Putting aside her shortcomings, she stepped away from the bench and asked, "What do you think?"

"Looks good," he replied, eyes twinkling in fun. "You're hired."

"You already hired me, remember?"

"I remember. Best personnel decision I ever made."

"Thank you." Dipping into a mock curtsy, she grinned up at him. "We're a good team."

"Yeah, we are."

His voice had a mellow tinge to it, and the blue in his eyes gradually shifted to a color

even a master artist would have trouble match-
ing. Caught up in the warmth of his gaze, she
wondered what she could have possibly done
to bring it on. Just as she was about to ask,
Chase and Cody came racing over to bookend
her between them.

"Mom, can I spend the night at Cody's?"

Cody's very pregnant mother, Sharon, was
close behind them, and she laughed. "Guys, I
was going to ask. Remember?"

"You're too slow," Cody informed her im-
patiently.

"Can't argue with that," she said, patting
her rounded waist with a smile. "Anyway,
Chase is welcome to come home with us if
he wants. He can borrow some clothes from
Cody, and I'll make sure they both get to summer rec in the morning."

In light of her earlier musings about returning to Boston, Holly wondered if it was a good
idea for her son to become more attached to a
friend he'd be leaving behind so soon. Then
again, life was short, and she was a firm be-
liever in enjoying every minute of it. "It's fine
with me. You've got my cell number if you
need me for anything."

"Sure do. I'm dead on my feet, so we're
heading home now. Have a good night."

"You, too," Holly replied, watching the patient woman trail after the much-faster boys. Sharon said something to them, and Chase spun around to wave.

"'Bye, Mom! See you tomorrow.'"

Holly waved back, trying not to be bothered by the casual way he'd trotted away from her. It wasn't that long ago that he refused to let go of her hand at the playground, and before this he'd never even considered spending the night anywhere other than home. She was proud of her little man, but she couldn't help feeling a bit wistful about the tagalong boy she'd loved since before he was born.

Other families began getting ready to leave, so she decided the painting would be her last task for the night. Once she'd finished, Sam helped her clean out the brushes and stow them in the equipment shed he'd built nearby. He snapped the combination lock closed and turned to survey the empty fields.

After several moments, she followed his line of sight but didn't see anything that would hold his attention for so long. "Is something wrong?"

"Just thinking."

"About what?"

"Nate," he confessed quietly. To her surprise, rather than the frown that usually accompanied thoughts of his friend, a smile creased Sam's weathered features. "He really loved playing baseball, and he was great with kids. He would've been the first one to sign up for this project."

Holly wasn't sure how to respond, and then inspiration struck. "We should name the field after him."

"Henderson Field," Sam said, testing out how it sounded. "I like it."

"If you build the frame, I'll design the logo and get it painted. We can dedicate the fields at the first practice on Monday."

"That'd be great."

He was still gazing into the distance, and instinct told her that it was time to discover once and for all what was plaguing Sam Calhoun.

"Sam?"

She got absolutely no response, and she feared he'd gotten snared in whatever memories this beautiful piece of land held for him. It took her a couple more tries, but she finally got his attention. Once he was focused on her, she summoned every ounce of her patience. "Tell me what happened to Nate."

His entire body stiffened as if she'd physically attacked him, and he made an obvious effort to relax. But the rigid set of his jaw told her that while his muscles had relaxed, his emotions were another issue. "I did."

"What really happened. I understand him leaving you his truck, but you drive it as if it still belongs to him and you're just borrowing it for the day. You have to admit, it's pretty unusual, and I don't mind telling you it worries me."

"You've got enough to worry about."

"So don't add to the list." Edging closer, she rested a comforting hand on his arm. In her gentlest voice, she said, "Please tell me what happened."

Sam's eyes met hers, filled with such anguish, she wished she'd kept her mouth shut. She hated to put him through this, but her gut was telling her that it was the best thing she could do to help the man who'd been so good to her family.

"No one knows," he murmured. "I've never told anyone."

Why? she nearly asked, but she held it in check because it really didn't matter why. What mattered was that he was clearly ready to confide in her, and she wanted to make it as easy as possible for him. So she sat down on a bench and gave him an encouraging smile. "Go ahead, Sam. I'm listening."

Anxiety flared in his eyes, but they didn't

take on that cautionary steel color she'd learned to be wary of. Instead, they went a murky bluish gray that was gloomy but not threatening. After sitting next to her, he heaved a bone-weary sigh, closed his eyes and dropped his head in shame.

"Nate died because of me."

Holly's instinct was to blurt out a definitive no, assure him that whatever had gone on in that battle wasn't his fault. But she sensed that was the last thing he needed, so she opted for rubbing his tense shoulders in a supportive gesture.

Lifting his head, he angled a disbelieving look at her. "Didn't you hear what I said?"

"I heard you," she replied gently, stilling her hand to avoid aggravating him further.

"And you're still sitting here with me?"

Holly chanced a smile. "I'm waiting for you to finish your story."

The stern set of his jaw eased a bit, and he shook his head. "You're nuts, you know that?"

She recognized an attempt to put her off when she heard one, and she decided the best parry was to remain silent. After what felt like a very long time, he finally seemed to realize that she wasn't going to let him off the hook, and in a halting voice he began.

"I'll spare you the gory details, but we got

pinned down during an ambush, and Nate couldn't walk on his own. We couldn't reach our unit on the radio, so it was just the two of us, and no one knew where we were. He wasn't too bad, so we decided he'd be okay while I backtracked to get a medic. Someone must've been hidden nearby and saw me leave. They knew he was vulnerable, and they—" Sam paused, swallowing hard enough that she could almost feel the strangling emotion herself. "When I got back, he was dead."

"Oh, Sam," she murmured, gently rubbing his clenched shoulders. She knew there was nothing she could do to ease his suffering, and that helplessness made her want to cry. For the struggling soldier, for Brady—for all the men and women who made it home but discovered that as much as they wanted to return to the lives they'd left behind, it simply wasn't possible.

Somehow, they had to trudge forward on paths they hadn't chosen, fighting their way through the darkness to reclaim a semblance of what they'd once had. Watching this brave, tortured man go through his ordeal again humbled her in a way she'd never experienced. At first, she didn't know what else to say. And then she did, and she thanked God for giving her the words she needed.

"You brought him home so his parents could lay him to rest," she reminded him. "I'm sure that means a lot to them."

"That's what they said to me after they buried him," Sam replied in a voice laced with the weariness of someone who'd lived that day over and over in his head. "I still don't get it."

Something about the way he phrased the revelation struck her oddly. It took her a few moments, but then she realized why. "Did you go to his funeral?"

Grimacing, Sam shook his head. "My family went, but I just couldn't do it."

"Have you been to his grave?"

He clenched his teeth so hard, she could hear them grinding together. "No."

"It might help," she suggested as gently as she could. "It would give you a chance to say goodbye."

"I don't want to."

Holly knew she was treading on very dangerous ground, and she chose her words with great care. "Did you ever consider the idea that if you did, you might be able to move past what happened and—"

"And what? Forget about my best friend?"

"Of course not, but you need to get back to living your own life instead of constantly punishing yourself for Nate's death." He wasn't buying her argument, so she tried another approach. "Nate was a soldier, and a Ranger besides. He knew the risks he was taking in serving his country, but he did it, anyway. Do you honestly believe he'd want you to blame yourself for something you had no control over?"

"I could've stayed with him."

"And then you'd both be dead." She met his furious gaze with a stubborn one of her own. "I don't think Nate would've wanted that. Do you?"

"No." The reply came on a frustrated breath, and Sam gave her a melancholy look that would have melted a heart much harder than hers. "I hear what you're saying, but I don't know how to make it happen."

"We'll name the field after him," she suggested again. "But in the meantime, let's take a drive."

Another deep sigh, as if he knew what was coming next. "To the cemetery?"

"Yes. I'll go to the site with you if you want."

"I don't want to go at all."

She knew she'd pushed him much further than was reasonable, but she was proud of how far he'd come and wasn't about to let him backslide now. But since she wasn't heartless, she stood and held out her hand. "Do you trust me?"

He stared at her hand for a couple of seconds, then took it lightly in his and lifted his eyes to hers in the most courageous gesture she'd ever seen. "Yeah, I do."

"I honestly believe that accepting what happened to Nate is the best way for you to begin healing. You need to go and say goodbye to him."

"Did doing that help you when Brady died?"

"Not at first," she confided sadly. "I hated him for giving up on himself and our family. All those contrived grieving steps made me want to scream, but I made myself go through them because I had a little boy who needed his mom to be strong. After a while, with time and a lot of faith, I found some peace, and I know you can, too. But you have to start somewhere."

With a gentle tug, she got him moving toward the truck he drove in honor of the friend he'd lost so tragically. As they headed down the lane that led toward the Liberty Creek Cemetery, she prayed that she was right.

Because if she wasn't, she feared that Sam would never be able to escape his past.

* * *

It didn't take them long to find Nate's resting place.

The Henderson area of the cemetery occupied a small hill beneath a stand of trees that had probably been there for a hundred years. Since it was mid-July, the branches overhead shaded the ground, the leaves rustling as a breeze drifted through them. Sam couldn't help thinking that they were sighing at him for staying away so long.

Nate's modest stone wasn't anything special, but the American flag displayed beside it made the humble marker stand out from the others around it. The wind ruffled the flag, carrying it up so the stripes rested over top of the arched granite. Without thinking, Sam reached out to smooth it back down to where it had started. The fabric was soft to the touch, and he let it slip through his fingers in a waterfall of red, white and blue.

Holly didn't say anything, but he could sense her presence behind him, watching over him protectively. While Sam had plenty of family to lean on, the battle he'd been fighting had been mostly his alone. Now that he'd confided the truth to her, it was nice to know she had his back.

Staring down at the mute stone, he struggled to connect the somber view with the fun-loving goofball who'd been his best friend since childhood. He couldn't manage it, and while he mulled over what that meant, the wind kicked up and blew his hair into his eyes. As he brushed it back, he understood why this place didn't speak to him.

Nate wasn't here.

His body might have been laid to rest in this peaceful spot, but the raucous spirit of his friend wasn't something that could be contained in the ground. It lived on with his family and friends, people who'd known and loved him. And for Sam, it lingered at the baseball fields and in the truck Nate had left to him, a reminder of the adventures they'd enjoyed together before fate had separated them so completely.

Glancing around at the somber view, Sam expected to feel that old darkness creeping back into his thoughts. He was surprised to discover that, while he didn't exactly feel upbeat, he wasn't overwhelmed by grief, either. Somehow, coming here seemed to have released some of the guilt he'd been carrying around with him for so long. It struck him as odd, and he turned to Holly.

"I'm not sure what's going on, but I don't feel as bad as I thought I would."

"I'm glad to hear that," she told him, adding a warm, encouraging smile. "You've been through so much, I wasn't sure how this would go."

"Then why'd you drag me up here?"

"Because you needed to come," she replied in a firm tone that told him she knew what she was talking about, "and I didn't want you to do it alone."

"Mom's been trying to get me to come up here for months," he confessed with a frown. "I just couldn't make myself do it."

"You weren't ready then. Now you are."

"But how did you know that?" he pressed, amazed that she could possibly understand him so well.

"You told me what really happened that day," she explained patiently, resting a comforting hand over the tags dangling down his chest. "That can't have been easy to do, but you were finally able to get the words out. The first time is always the hardest."

This woman had endured more than her share of anguish, he knew, and he admired her willingness to reach out and help him in such a personal way. Resting his hand over hers, he gave her a grateful smile. "Thanks for being here, Holly. I couldn't have done it without you."

She gazed up at him, those beautiful blue eyes shining in the dappled sunlight filtering through the branches overhead. The smile she gave him made him glad he'd opened up to her. "I think you could have, but I'm glad you let me come along." After a moment, she tilted her head with a questioning look. "Why did you?"

"You dragged me by the arm," he reminded her with a chuckle. "Remember?"

Groaning, she rolled her eyes in disdain. "Oh, please. You're twice my size, and I can hardly push you around. This is the kind of thing people normally do in private or with family. I'm curious why you chose me."

Now that she mentioned it, so was he. He wasn't a hermit, but he wasn't one for public displays of emotion, good or bad. He tried to keep a more or less even keel, moving from one day to the next at a steady pace that kept his business on track. Even he recognized that he'd put more personal things on the back burner, waiting for some day in the future when he felt strong enough to pull them forward and deal with them.

When it occurred to him that their hands were still connected, he gently folded hers into his, brushing a kiss over the back. "I guess it just felt like the right thing to do."

A smile slowly made its way across her features, brightening them in a way that made him happy to know he'd been the one to put it there. "I'm glad."

"Yeah," he agreed with a smile of his own. "Me, too."

After a long look down at Nate's grave, Sam put an arm around her shoulders and turned to go. Not wanting her to feel crowded, he began to pull his arm free but was pleased when she slid her arms around his waist and held him close. Sweet and trusting, the gesture warmed him down to the soles of his boots, and he found himself wishing it could be the first of many moments like this between them.

Walking down the hill was easier than the hike up, and with each step he felt lighter, as if he was shedding some of the weight he'd been lugging around in his heart. People had tried to do that for him in the past, but he'd always rejected their attempts, insisting on carrying the load by himself. Now that he'd shared some of it with her, the burden seemed a lot easier to bear.

For all her delicate looks, Holly had impressed him more than once with the steel that seemed to run through her. The silver cross she wore glinted in the sunlight, and he wondered if she was right that the first step in forgiving himself was to forgive God for not intervening on that terrible day. Too many times, he'd heard the platitudes about God's will and how people had to learn to accept things they didn't understand. In the past, those sentiments had infuriated him to the point where he'd turned his back on the faith he'd been raised with.

Somehow, Holly had found a way to make peace with the Almighty. Maybe there was hope for him to do it, too.

Chapter Eleven

Finally.

After weeks of hard work and crossed fingers, Henderson Field was ready for the first game. And not a moment too soon, as far as Chase was concerned. Holly had barely pried her eyes open when he bounced into her room, his new cleats clunking on the hardwood floor.

"Morning, Mom!" he sang, bounding onto her bed with the kind of energy she would've paid almost anything to have for herself. "It's a great day for baseball."

Squinting at the weak sunshine streaming into her windows, she couldn't help laughing. "I can't argue with that. What time is it?"

"Seven." Holly knew him pretty well, and she gave him a long look that made him grin. "Okay, it's almost seven."

"Meaning more like six?"

"In between," he hedged, well aware that she knew he could tell time. "I don't wanna be late for warm-ups."

The game started at nine, so there wasn't much danger of him missing anything. But she didn't want to squash his enthusiasm, so she flung the covers aside and got up. "Good point. I'll get breakfast going while you wake up D. She wants to come with us, and it'll take her a while to get ready."

"Okay."

He zoomed off on his errand, and she followed him downstairs, feeling a bit more energetic with each step. He stopped just long enough to let Holly fill a tray with his usual breakfast and Daphne's morning tea. To Holly's surprise, when she knocked on the parlor door, Daphne called out, "Come in!"

She wasn't what you'd call a morning person, so Holly was amazed to find her sitting on her love seat, hair done and makeup on. Pleased but concerned, Holly set down the tray and said, "You know you're not supposed to be in the shower by yourself."

"Then why did Sam install those grab bars for me?" Daphne countered in a maddeningly logical tone. Smiling proudly, she patted Holly's arm. "You're sweet to worry, but I managed just fine on my own. I had my phone with me in case I needed you."

Despite the difficulty she'd had adjusting to their new relationship, Holly couldn't help feeling proud of her mother for taking back some of the independence she'd always cherished. Being pampered was one thing, Holly knew. Being a step short of helpless was something else entirely, and she was glad to see that Daphne had finally had enough of that. "Well, that was smart. When you're done eating, let me know if you want a hand getting dressed."

"Will do," her patient promised, the spark in those famous eyes making it clear that she had no intention of giving up so easily.

Chase found one of his favorite cartoons, and when Holly left, the two of them were already imitating the goofy main character, laughing more at each other than at the ridiculous scene on the TV.

Apparently, their attitude was contagious because Holly was singing along with the kitchen radio when she heard a quiet knock on the wooden frame of the screen door. Glancing over, she saw Sam silhouetted there, thermos in one hand and a large white bag in the other.

"Breakfast delivery," he said, holding up what he'd brought.

"Anyone who brings me food can come right on in," she told him, taking a long sniff as he stepped inside. "That smells amazing."

"Fresh outta the oven. Don't worry—Gran made the coffee," he joked with a grin.

The lighthearted reference to their first meeting, when she nearly choked on his turbo-charged brew, caught her by surprise. It had happened weeks ago, but she never would have suspected that the somber former Ranger she met that day would be capable of poking fun at himself. She didn't want to make him feel awkward by mentioning that, so instead she smiled back. "Please thank her for us."

"You can tell her yourself," he replied as he poured them each a cup of steaming caffeine. "She'll be there today."

"At the game? Why?"

"To cheer the kids on. It's the first one, and she knows most of them, so she wants to be there."

Holly had never heard of such a thing. In Boston, people had been so busy with their own hectic lives, they often couldn't make it to their own kids' games. It was drop off, run errands or go back to the office, then pick them up. And carpooling was part of the parents' survival kit, so no one had to drive back and forth every time.

"You look like I just told you she's going to the moon for lunch," Sam teased, handing Holly's cup to her.

"It's just that I wouldn't expect someone to come this morning when they don't have a child or grandchild involved."

"Well, she's gotten attached to Chase," Sam explained, taking a seat at the table. Glancing down the short hallway toward Daphne's closed door, in a lower voice he said, "She thinks it's a shame his own grandma's in Georgia so she can't be here to see him play. Gran thought it'd be nice if she was there instead."

"You're not going to shame me into telling him about Daphne," Holly shot back in a furious whisper. "I'll do it when I think the time's right."

Sitting back, Sam studied her for several long, uncomfortable moments, his eyes shifting through several shades of blue to almost gray, then back again. It was the most incredible thing she'd ever seen, and if she hadn't known him as well as she did, the eerie shifts would have made her skin crawl.

"You're gonna wait till you're gone, aren't you?"

There was no anger in his tone, only a quiet

resignation that suggested he understood what she was thinking. Holly had never met anyone who followed her thoughts so easily, and while it made explaining herself easier, she wasn't sure she liked it. "I may. I haven't decided yet."

Apparently convinced that he was getting precisely nowhere, he didn't say anything more on the subject. Smart man.

"So," he went on as if they hadn't just had a tangle of opinions, "what's next for you two?"

"Now that I've gotten away, I'm definitely not going back to the same area of Boston. I don't want to uproot Chase once he's settled in a school and making friends, so this move has to be it for a long time. Savannah was a possibility before—y'know," she replied, sighing as she sat down next to him. "Now I'm not sure."

"Are you considering staying here?"

"No," she answered reflexively. "That's not an option right now. Maybe not ever." The frustration she'd been keeping at bay ever since she learned her family's secret bubbled to the surface, and she waved her hands in an attempt to keep it under wraps. "I just don't know."

"You don't have to know," he told her in a gentle tone that told her he truly sympathized with how she was feeling. "Just do whatever's best for you and Chase, and you'll be fine."

"You sound a lot more confident than I feel."

"You've been following your gut since he was born," Sam reminded her with a smile. "He's a terrific kid, so from where I sit, it's working well so far. No reason to think that won't continue."

Gratitude flooded her heart, and she gave him her brightest smile. "Thank you for saying that."

"You're welcome." Looking down, he fiddled with the handle on his cup before meeting her eyes again. "So Chase is headed into third grade, but how 'bout you? When school starts next month, you'll have a lot of time to fill. Any thoughts on what kind of job you're looking for when you get settled?"

Holly opened her mouth to answer, then quickly changed her mind. When he gave her a nudging look, she stalled. "It's silly."

"Try me."

The sketches she'd done for the living room were stacked on the table, and she fingered the pile while she debated confiding her insane idea to him. Why not? she wondered. The worst he could do was laugh and tell her to get real. The moment that possibility entered her mind, she dismissed it. That was how Brady would have reacted, forcing her to backpedal and be more pragmatic.

But Sam would never cut her down that way, even if he thought she was nuts. As he'd done with the Japanese garden out back, she was certain that he'd listen and do his best to support her. Even if what she wanted made no sense to him. Because that was the kind of guy he was.

Whether it was signing on to Brian's plans for the ironworks or working long hours to make sure local kids had a place to play baseball and softball, she'd learned that while the reserved contractor was as practical as they came, he did all he could to help others make their dreams come true.

After a deep breath, she decided there was no harm in entrusting her wild notion to the stalwart man she'd come to admire so much. "Okay, but you can't tell anyone else."

"Promise."

"I've really enjoyed working on this house," she began, fanning the drawings out with her fingertip. "I know D isn't a real client, but she's always liked my ideas, and working with you has been fun."

That got her a quick smile. "Thanks. I feel the same about working with you."

Really? After all their rehab debates and outright arguments, Holly figured he'd view her as demanding and impossible to please. Just another way he differed from—well, any other man she'd ever known. Putting that aside, she refocused on what she'd been saying. Another deep breath, and she blurted out, "So I was thinking maybe I could take some classes and become a bona fide interior designer."

Nothing.

Sam regarded her with a pensive expression, as if he was trying to decide how to let her down easily. Then, to her amazement, he nodded. "Sounds perfect for you. If you need a portfolio of work you've done, I've got plenty of before and after pictures of this place."

Holly hadn't gotten past the breathless wishing phase of her evolving plan, and his pragmatic suggestion made her heart skip. "I never even thought of that. What a fabulous suggestion."

"Yeah, I get 'em once in a while. You can use me as a reference, and I can't imagine anyone else in the program will have a movie star as their first client. That should impress your professors."

"On-campus classes would be the same

time that Chase is in school," she said, her enthusiasm growing with each word, "and maybe they have some online, too."

"I'd imagine so."

Wary of letting her imagination take off with her common sense, Holly tried to calm her racing heart. "Do you really think I could make it work?"

"Is it what you want?"

"Yes," she replied without hesitation. She was so accustomed to examining every decision she made in excruciating detail, and the delay often left her not deciding anything at all. Which, of course, meant that nothing ever changed.

Until the day when Daphne called and asked for her help while recovering from her back injury. Holly had instantly agreed because there was nothing she wouldn't do for the woman who'd been such a bright, exciting influence on her since she was a child. Even now, Holly knew that adjusting to her new role as Daphne Mills's daughter was only a matter of time. Because when all was said and done, she loved Daphne to pieces and would find a way past the jarring revelation that had changed so much in an instant.

"You sounded like your mom just now," Sam told her, adding that slightly crooked grin she'd come to appreciate more and more. "I think there's a lot of dreamer in you, whether you want to see it or not."

"I think you're right," she agreed, tapping empty cups with him. "But for now, I'm hungry. What did Ellie send us?"

"One of everything that was ready," he replied, motioning to the bag. "Ladies first."

"Meaning you snagged one on your way here," she accused, pulling out a huge sample that appeared to be the size of an actual bear's paw.

He chuckled while he refilled their cups from the thermos. "Busted. But in my defense, they smelled too good to resist, and I was starving."

"You're forgiven. This time," she added, sending him a threatening look that only made him grin.

As they finished off their meal, they talked through the logistics of college classes for Holly, what she was looking for in a school for Chase, and the extra touches the league wanted to put on the fields for next season. Everything, she noticed, but one topic that had suddenly become very sensitive.

Where would Holly be starting this new life of hers? She knew from experience that summers in New England zipped by and turned into fall before she could blink. With Chase starting school in September, they had to be settled soon to give them time to acclimate to a new place and get her registered for the design classes she was so excited about.

All that meant leaving Liberty Creek and the friends they'd both made here. And while Holly was confident that Daphne would support whatever choice she made, she suspected that leaving the mother she'd just discovered wouldn't be easy for her to do. And then, she was stunned to hear a tiny voice whispering in the back of her mind.

What about Sam?

He'd come to mean so much to Chase, and Holly didn't know how her son would react to leaving his tall buddy behind. Then in her next thought, she realized that she was going to miss him, too. Apparently, despite her best efforts to maintain a healthy distance from the former soldier, he'd come to mean more to her than she'd realized.

That was going to make leaving Liberty Creek a lot tougher than she'd anticipated.

These kids were awesome.

Sam had great memories of playing baseball when he was young, but nothing compared to watching Chase, Cody and their teammates in their very first organized game. For the kids with no prior experience, a coach set the ball on a pitching machine for them so they'd have a chance at getting a hit. But when his turn came around, Chase stepped to the plate and boldly asked for a live pitcher. And not just any of the dads standing along the sideline, either.

"Sam can do it. He pitches to me all the time at home," he announced as if it had never occurred to him to request anyone else.

"I really just came to watch," Sam hedged, wishing he was small enough to fade into the crowd. The fact that Holly was smothering a laugh didn't escape him, and he wondered if this had been her idea.

Before he could ask her about it, Chase turned hopeful eyes on him. "Please?"

There was no vetoing that kind of plea, so Sam took the low mound and threw a few practice pitches before grooving one down the center of the plate. Chase hit a double into the outfield and then Cody cracked one over the center fielder's head, driving them both around to score. After that, everyone on both teams decided to give live pitching a try.

Unfortunately, most of them couldn't hit a watermelon with their light metal bats, which left Sam piling up a lot of full counts and endless foul balls. Tiring as it was, though, he was surprised to discover that he was having a blast. The teams were coed, and he registered the fact that the girls sprinkled throughout the rosters were better at defense, while the boys excelled at offense.

When he mentioned that to Holly, she tilted her head in a curious pose. "You're right. I wonder why that is."

"Girls are smarter?" he suggested, getting a bright laugh in reply.

"Are you trying to butter me up for something? Because I have to warn you, Chase has perfected that approach, so I'm pretty much immune."

"Nah, that's Brian's gig. If I want something, I'll just tell you straight out."

It wasn't like him to be so direct with a woman, and he cringed when he considered how that might sound to her. To his immense relief, she just smiled. "I'll keep that in mind."

The smile reached into her eyes, making them sparkle like gems in the sunlight. Was it his imagination, or was there a warmth in them he hadn't seen there before? Could it be that he'd finally found a woman who could accept him as he was, scars and all? While he had to admit that was possible, the idea prompted another question that was harder for him to answer.

What was he going to do about it?

With Daphne nearly back at full strength and the school year they'd discussed earlier fast approaching, Holly and Chase would be leaving town sooner rather than later. While Sam would love for them to stay longer, he'd never ask the young widow to put aside her dream of a fresh start to be with him. She'd sacrificed enough of her life to someone else, putting off what she wanted to take care of Brady.

Then again, there were perfectly good elementary and high schools right here in Liberty Creek, and while he didn't know much about interior design, he suspected that she could take those classes at the small college over in Waterford.

Did he dare suggest that to her? What if he did, and she shot down the notion? Even more troubling, what if she decided it sounded good to her? If she put off her leaving and things didn't work out between them, she and Chase would have to switch schools partway through the year, which was always more problematic for students compared to those who started at a school in the beginning of the year. The other alternative of her staying and things going great between them was appealing to him but didn't seem all that likely. Like Brian resurrecting the family business, a successful relationship between Sam and Holly was dicey, at best.

Sam was a hands-on kind of guy, and he took pride in building things to last. He wasn't keen on taking that leap with Holly, only to have it all fall apart in a few months. And he was fairly certain she felt the same way. Not only for herself, but for Chase, who deserved a real father, not one who faded from his life because the guy wasn't ready for that kind of responsibility.

Looking around at the families gathered for the game, Sam couldn't help noticing how happy they seemed. Parents wore the T-shirts of their children's teams, shouting encouragement and pointing to where the current play was. Younger kids were playing along the sidelines, picking flowers and rolling in the grass while they munched on snacks.

It looked nice to him, but he was standing at a distance from it all. He'd only just begun to feel comfortable in his own skin again, and he wasn't sure about taking on anything more than he already had. For the first time, it dawned on him that in allowing himself to get so close to the Andrewses, he was on the verge of doing something he tried very hard never to do: make a commitment he wasn't sure he could keep.

"Sam?"

Holly's voice dragged him from his brooding, and he gladly focused on her. "Yeah?"

"The coach asked if you want to pitch another inning." Worry dimmed those beautiful eyes, and she rubbed his arm in the comforting motion she'd used with him more times than he could recall. "Are you okay?"

"Fine."

Stepping closer, she said, "Are you sure? You looked like you were somewhere else just now."

This woman could read him so well, it scared him sometimes. Knowing that she'd come by that skill nursing someone who'd finally given up made him sick inside. Worry had been an element of Holly's life for so long, it seemed to have become part of who she was. She deserved better than that.

And Sam wanted her to have it. So he plastered a smile on his face and forced a positive tone. "Never better."

He ignored her suspicious look and picked up his glove, waving it toward Chase's coach. As he trotted toward the mound, Holly called out his name. Turning, he saw her holding up his vintage Red Sox cap. Apparently, he'd left it on the bench, and she came onto the field to return it to him.

Standing on tiptoe so she could reach, she settled it on his head, smiling as she tapped the brim. "I thought you might want this to keep the sun out of your eyes."

"Thanks."

It was a simple thing, no big deal, he told himself as she went back to her spot on the sidelines and he continued to the mound. But the fact that she'd thought of what he wanted touched him in a way he'd never felt before, deep down in a place no other woman had ever found her way into. And that was when he knew.

He'd gone and fallen in love with Holly Andrews.

The kicker was that he couldn't even tell her how he felt because knowing her she'd put aside her plans and stay in town so they could be together.

Much as he wished things could be different, they weren't. And in spite of how far he'd come, there was nothing he could do about it.

Sunday morning, Daphne was feeling so much better that Holly served their breakfast in the freshly painted dining room. The huge oval table felt odd with just the three of them, its deep cherry color polished to a mirror finish that would have passed muster in any mansion in the country. But once she added place settings and Oliver Chesterton's most recent vase of flowers, it felt like any other meal she'd shared with her famous relative.

"This is just beautiful, Holly," her mother said, adding a warm smile while she poured real maple syrup onto her Belgian waffle. "And it smells wonderful, too."

"Good pancakes, Mom," Chase chimed in, plopping a fresh one onto his plate. "Papa was right—this is the best syrup ever."

"Papa?" Daphne echoed curiously. "Who's that?"

"Cody's grandpa. He said everyone calls him Papa, so I could, too. He's really nice."

"Yes, he is. You've made a lot of friends here in Liberty Creek this summer. What are their plans for the fall?"

While they chatted about his collection of new buddies, several expressions crossed Daphne's face, alerting Holly to the fact that something important was going on behind those famed violet eyes. She couldn't imagine what it might be, but she wasn't surprised when her mom said, "Chase, I'd like some grown-up talk with your mother. Could you give us a few minutes?"

She spoke to him as if he was an adult himself instead of eight, and Holly smothered a grin when he blinked in response. Clearly confused, he stared across the table at her, waiting for her to interpret. "It looks like you're done, so why don't you take your dishes into the kitchen and go get ready for church?"

"Ohhh. Okay." Standing, he carefully picked up his dishes and left the canyon of a dining room.

Once she heard him banging around in the bathroom upstairs, she turned to her mother expectantly. "That should buy us about ten minutes. What's up?"

"I know you have to make your plans soon," she started in immediately, telling Holly she'd been thinking about whatever she wanted to say for a while now. "I just want you to know that if you and Chase would enjoy staying here in Liberty Creek, you're more than welcome to stay here. With me," she added, as if she worried that the detail was necessary.

Hesitating, Holly took a sip of her coffee before saying, "That's very generous of you. Thank you for the offer."

"Oh, that's just nonsense," the diva spat, obviously offended. "We've known each other your entire life. There's no need to be so polite with me, Peaches. If you want to stay, there's plenty of space here for you both. If not, you're just as welcome to leave. I know you're anxious to be away from your old neighborhood, and I just wanted you to know you have an option other than moving to a strange place where you don't know anyone."

There was more to it, Holly knew, but the stubborn woman was too proud to do anything even remotely like begging. Leaning closer, she murmured, "I'm sorry to make you angry, D. I haven't made any decisions yet, even though I really should've by now." Reaching out, she patted a manicured hand in the same gesture she'd received many times herself. "Maybe it's because if we go, we'll miss you, too."

In a heartbeat, tears flooded her mercurial mother's eyes, accompanied by a hopeful look that would have broken a heart much softer than Holly's. "Do you mean that?"

"Absolutely. It was tough for me at first, finding out you're my mother, wondering why things went the way they did. I hated not having a say in it, and being kept in the dark so long made me furious." Hearing the edge on her tone, Holly took a moment to regain her composure to make sure she kept her voice down. "But once I got over the shock, I believed you when you said you did it out of love. You've never been anything but wonderful to me, and I love you to pieces. I still wish you could've been honest about everything sooner, but there's no changing the past. All we can do is move forward the way we are and hope for the best."

"Does that mean you forgive me?"

Did it? Holly wondered, rolling the question around in her mind. She didn't want to knee-jerk something this important and discover later that she'd just been caught up in the dramatic moment and said something she couldn't reverse later. Because her brain was useless in situations like this, she took a chance and let her heart speak for her. "Yes, I forgive you."

"Oh, I love the sound of that," she said in a voice filled with genuine emotion. Covering Holly's hand with hers, she added a grateful smile. "Thank you. I don't deserve your forgiveness, but you have no idea how much it means to me to have it. I was beginning to wonder if my decision to keep the truth from you would haunt me forever."

The words struck a chord with Holly, and she frowned. "I don't want that to happen with Chase."

"Then tell him, sooner rather than later. Trust me—it only gets harder the longer you wait."

Her advice echoed what Sam had advised her to do more than once, and Holly figured that if two people she admired felt the same way, she'd do well to listen. "I guess there's no time like the present. Chase, come down here, please!"

A few moments later, he came thundering down the front stairway, his white button-down shirt untucked and only one good shoe on. When she saw him, she couldn't help laughing. "I could've waited until you were done getting dressed."

"You don't yell much, so I thought it was important."

"It is." Exchanging nervous looks with her mom, Holly focused back on him. "We have something to tell you. About our family."

Fear flooded his eyes, and he dropped into a chair. "Is someone sick?"

"No," Holly reassured him instantly, feeling awful for bringing up the specter of Brady's illness. Summoning all her patience, she knelt beside her son's chair and tried to keep it simple. "A long time ago, Auntie D was planning to marry someone in England. His name was

Ian, and you've seen pictures of him with his race car."

"Sure. What about him?"

There was no easy way to explain it, so Holly opted for the direct approach. "Not long ago, I learned that he was my father. And Auntie D is my mother."

Understandably, Chase's features twisted in confusion as his young mind attempted to wrap itself around a secret that had flustered her for weeks. Clearly seeking answers, he swung his gaze to the anxious woman at the head of the table. "So you're my grandma?"

"Yes, honey."

"Why didn't you tell me?"

Holly understood that reaction all too well, but she thought it best to let Daphne answer in her own way. This was between her and Chase.

"As your mother said," she began hesitantly, "it was a long time ago. Ian and I were planning to get married, but he was killed in a racing accident before our wedding. I wanted my baby to have a real family, with a mother and father, and siblings to grow up with. I couldn't give her those things, so my sister and I agreed that it was best if she and her husband adopt your mom and raise her." Giv-

254 *Mending the Widow's Heart*

ing Holly a proud smile, she added, "I think they did a marvelous job."

Chase seemed totally lost, and he shook his head as if trying to sort out the puzzle she'd presented him. "Who are Gramma and Grampa?"

"Your great-aunt and uncle," Holly explained. "Aunt Cara and Aunt Julie are actually my cousins, so they're your cousins, too."

While he chewed on that, he studied Daphne with an expression way too somber for someone his age. "You lied to Mom because you loved her?"

She blinked in surprise, then let out a short laugh. "I never thought of it that way, but I guess that's about the size of it."

His baffled gaze swung to Holly. "And you told me the truth because you love me."

Uh-oh, Holly thought. This was a sticky one. "Well, yes."

"Grown-ups are weird."

"Yes, they are." Laughing, she hugged him, immensely relieved to discover that her son seemed to be taking the life-altering news much better than she'd anticipated. Maybe Sam was right and Chase had inherited her resilience rather than his father's surrendering nature.

"Mom?"

Holding him at arm's length, she said, "Yes?"

He held out the uneven hem of his new shirt. "There's a lot of buttons on this, and I missed one. Can you help me?"

"I sure can."

As she unbuttoned them and redid them, his innocent question echoed in her mind, making her smile.

Can you help me?

Those few simple words reminded her of the time not long ago when Sam had asked her the same thing. The situation had been very different, but knowing that the former soldier trusted her enough to ask had made her feel the way she did right now.

Content.

Sunday morning, Sam woke up before his usual time. He'd set his alarm a little earlier for today because he had an important errand to run. After dressing in his nicest clothes, he slipped off Nate's dog tags and studied the dulled metal pieces that had hung around his neck—and his heart—for more than a year.

Glancing at the photo of Nate and him that he still kept on his dresser, for the first time in recent memory, Sam smiled when he recalled that day. Seniors in high school, they'd just won the league championship, and they were still grimy from a hard-fought victory but grinning like they'd taken game seven of the World Series.

"That was a great day," Sam said out loud, just in case Nate could hear him. "I'll always miss you and wish you were here. But I've gotta get on with my life, and I think this will help me do it. I hope you understand."

As he settled the tags into the cotton-lined box he'd gotten from Emma's jewelry studio, a peaceful sensation swept through him. Crazy as it seemed, Sam felt as if his message had been received in Heaven and Nate was letting him know he approved. Ever since he'd visited the cemetery with Holly, thoughts of his friend had crept in more and more often. Not the tormenting kind, but bright images of happy times they'd shared. There had been a lot of those, but when he'd been bogged down in the quagmire of his own guilt, those good memories had faded into the background of his mind. Now that they were front and center, he was hopeful that the worst of his ordeal was finally over.

But he had one more thing to do to set himself on the right path forward. It seemed so obvious to him now, he couldn't believe it hadn't occurred to him before. Before he could second-guess himself, he grabbed the box and hurried downstairs. In the driveway, the two trucks were parked side by side, as if offering him a choice: stay in the past or move into the future.

Suddenly doubting his plans, Sam toyed with his sturdy fob, staring down at each key in turn. While he'd kept up with the maintenance on his work truck, he hadn't cared much about it being clean, so it was a mess, inside and out. Nate's was much more presentable, and being practical, Sam angled his steps toward it. As he got closer, though, he noticed something.

The right front tire was flat.

He wasn't the fanciful type, but he could easily picture his old buddy giving him a shove away from the pain he'd been carting around for so long. Shooting a look into the sky, he laughed. "Okay, okay, I get it. You can stop now."

As a last-minute addition, he reached in for the box he'd used to haul favors for the parade and quickly filled it with all of Nate's things from the cab of the truck. It looked starkly empty without them, but he ignored the prick of doubt and checked to make sure he had everything. Satisfied, he set the small box on top and shut the door.

A run through the new automated car wash

took care of the worst of the grime on his own pickup, and Sam headed for Waterford. He parked at the curb next to a caboose-shaped mailbox that read *Henderson*. Determined to follow through on his task, he didn't hesitate but climbed out and went up the brick walkway to the front door.

He rang the bell, and almost immediately a woman's face appeared in one of the sidelights. When she saw him, her eyes widened in surprise and she flung open the door with a joyful look.

"Sam! It's so good to see you."

"Hi, Mrs. Henderson. I hope this isn't a bad time."

"Of course not," she assured him, stepping aside. "You just come right on in, and I'll let Peter know you're here."

Sam thanked her and stood in the foyer, unsure of what to do next. Through the archway that led into the living room, he saw Nate's formal Rangers portrait over the fireplace, a triangular framed flag sitting in the place of honor on the mantel. He'd been their only child, Sam recalled sadly, and now he was gone. He couldn't imagine how difficult it must be for parents to endure that kind of heartache.

Quick footsteps pulled him from his brooding, and he turned as a middle-aged man approached him, both hands held out for a warm handshake. "It's good to see you, son. How have you been?"

Normally, Sam would tell people he was fine and leave it at that, well aware that they knew it was far from the truth. But Holly had taught him that it was important to be honest, and that there was no shame in struggling, only in refusing to continue fighting. So he took a deep breath and said, "Better, thanks. Your new house is beautiful."

"That's Teresa's doing," the older man informed him, sending his wife a fond smile. "She's the decorator. I just sign the invoices."

"Do you want to come and sit?" she asked, motioning toward the living room.

The view in there was the last thing Sam needed when he was just beginning to regain his emotional balance. "No, thanks. I really just came by to give you these."

He held out what he'd brought, and by the look on Peter's face, he knew without looking what was inside the smaller one. Nate's father gave him a long, assessing look and finally nodded before taking the box from him. Teresa opened the jewelry box lid and dangled the tags the way Sam had done so often.

Bringing them to rest over her heart, she gave Sam a grateful smile. "Thank you."

"I didn't mean to keep them so long," he explained. "I thought about bringing them back a hundred times, but I just couldn't do it."

"What's different now?" she asked.

"I'm not sure," he confided, shrugging. "It just seemed like it was time."

Peter nodded, as if he'd heard something in Sam's response that made sense to him. Sam found himself wishing he understood it, too. Something more to work on, he supposed.

Catching himself, he halted the negative train of thought and forced himself to smile. "Well, I've got an appointment, so I need to get going. It was good to see you both again."

"Anytime, Sam," Teresa assured him, adding a warm hug. "You're always welcome here."

"Give our best to your family," Peter said as the three of them walked to the door.

"I will. Have a good day."

He went down the stairs, and this time the walkway didn't look half as long as it had when he first arrived. He even noticed what a beautiful morning it was. Sunny and warm, he mused as he started the engine and pulled away. A perfect day for new beginnings.

And he knew just where he was going to start.

The choir was warming up their voices when he slid into the conveniently vacant seat next to Holly. Clearly startled, she pulled away with a disgruntled look, ready to deliver a scolding. When she saw it was him, though, the glare mellowed into one of her beautiful smiles. "Good morning."

No comment about his rude exit a few weeks ago, Sam noticed, grinning as he returned the greeting. While he leaned over to read the news in the church bulletin she held, he pulled his collar aside to show her that he was missing something. She immediately grasped his meaning and whispered, "Where are they?"

"I drove over to Waterford and gave them back to Nate's parents, along with the stuff out of his truck. That's where they belong, anyway."

"Good for you." As if that wasn't enough, she reached around his back and cuddled him into a near-hug that was all the proof he needed that he'd done the right thing.

"And tomorrow, I'm dropping the truck off with Oliver's mechanic to get it repainted. I'm thinking burgundy would look nice."

"Not to mention it's more of a Red Sox color."

She really did get him, he thought with a grin as Chase snuck up the aisle and wedged himself into the corner next to Sam. "Cody and me think it's a good day for fishing."

"It always is," Sam agreed. "You wanna get through here?"

"Nah, this works for me."

Holly chuckled. "He sounded exactly like you just then."

"Is that a good thing?"

"Very good."

She punctuated her reply with a bright smile that made him wish for more of them. A lot more.

While the three of them sang along with the rest of the congregation, Sam glanced around and noticed that they looked like any other family there. Spending Sunday morning in God's house, surrounded by people who loved them, giving thanks for the blessings He'd brought into their lives. Sam couldn't recall ever feeling more peaceful than he did right this minute, and he sent up a silent prayer of thanks to the Almighty for having patience with him. Sam had tried everything he knew to shed his faith, but no matter how far away he drifted, God simply wouldn't let him go. The tragic nature of Nate's death hadn't changed, and neither had the fact that

Sam would miss him every day until they put him in the ground.

But in the past, he hadn't been sure that he could live with the sorrow of losing his best friend. Now, he knew he could. Because a plucky military widow from Savannah had shown him how. Staring at the portrait that hung behind the choir, he wondered if God had brought Holly to his very out-of-the-way hometown to rescue Sam from himself. Knowing that he needed a woman who saw him for who he was and understood, but who also wouldn't let him continue to drown in his grief.

He was still mulling that over when the song ended and everyone sat down. This sermon was a fitting metaphor about how life was like baseball, obviously aimed at the kids. Chase had been fidgeting while trying not to fidget, but at the mention of his favorite game, his leg-swinging stopped and he fixed his attention on the pastor.

Holly kept darting looks at him, and when those gorgeous blue eyes connected with Sam's, she rolled them in the kind of long-suffering look he'd seen so many times from his own mother.

"Boys," she muttered, shaking her head

with a fond smile that made it clear she actually didn't mind all that much.

When the smile deepened for him, Sam felt the same lurching sensation in his chest that he had at Chase's first game. This time, he recognized it for what it was, and he barely managed to swallow a groan of frustration. Ironically, it occurred to Sam that not long ago, he'd considered her intention to leave at the end of the summer to be the best thing for all of them.

But now, all he wanted was for her to stay.

Chapter Twelve

It was time to pack up and head for Boston.

Holly brought the last load of clean clothes upstairs and stopped in Chase's room to drop off his things. His suitcase lay open on the bed, mostly empty, while he was sprawled on the floor leafing through a baseball magazine that Sam had bought for him the other day. Chin on his hand while he skimmed through the pages filled with facts and player photos, he looked totally dejected.

She could relate, Holly thought with a grimace. Apparently, she wasn't the only one who was reluctant to leave the quaint, close-knit New Hampshire town that had begun to feel like home to both of them. It didn't feel quite right to her, but staying didn't, either. She'd come to terms with her decision, so her wishy-washy attitude bewildered her.

And that certainly didn't help her frame of mind any.

"Hey, bud," she greeted him, setting the basket on his bed to join him on the floor. Sitting cross-legged, she angled to see what he was looking at. "Is that the new Red Sox pitcher?"

"Yeah," Chase replied on a deep sigh. "Sam said they just brought him up from Pawtucket, and he's setting the league on fire."

That wasn't the kind of thing an eight-year-old would say, so Holly knew he was quoting their neighbor verbatim. Just as she'd feared when they'd first arrived, he'd gotten attached to Sam and now would be forced to say goodbye. This wasn't exactly the scenario she'd envisioned with such dread, but the result was the same.

Her son was heartbroken, and even though she'd gladly take the hurt away from him, she couldn't. Rubbing his back, she said, "I know you're sad about leaving, Chase, but we'll come back to visit. I promise."

"It won't be the same," he reminded her in a resigned tone. "Hanging out with Sam is kind of like—"

He stopped abruptly, clamping his mouth shut around something he obviously thought would upset her. But Holly had learned the hard way that it was worse to keep negative emotions bottled up, never knowing when they'd come shooting to the surface. So she dredged up a smile and nudged. "Like what?"

"Having a father," he finished in a rush, as if he couldn't keep the words in even a second longer. "Like my other friends in Boston did. Like Cody does. Sam and me like the same stuff, and he taught me a lot about how to build things. I think it'd be fun to do that for real someday."

Chase was a hands-on kid, always taking things apart to see how they worked and then putting them back together. Well, trying, anyway. There always seemed to be a few parts left over, but she encouraged him to do it because it made him happy. Replacing a few small appliances seemed like a small price to pay for nurturing his innate curiosity. "I think you'd be great at that, but you have plenty of time to decide what you're going to do when you're all grown up."

"I wanna be like Sam," her son announced confidently, eyes shining as he talked about his hero. "Big and strong, and always ready to help people when they need me."

Holly's mind instantly translated the childish goal into something more serious, and she swallowed back her terror so she could speak normally. "Those are good things to be."

"Not a soldier, though," he added somberly. "Because that would make you sad."

Unsure if she'd be able to talk without sobbing, she gathered him into her arms and held him tight. Just the thought of her only child being assigned to some far-off place where he'd be in harm's way made her crazy with fear. That he'd picked up on her reaction and chosen to protect her from that made her prouder of him than she'd ever been.

Grasping his arms, she held him away and gave him a smile full of gratitude. "Thank you for that, Chase. I can't tell you how much it means to me."

He tilted his head with a wary expression. "Are you gonna cry?"

"Maybe a little," she admitted with a laugh. "Because you just made me very happy."

Judging by his perplexed look, her explanation made absolutely no sense to him, but he politely avoided saying so. Instead, he glanced at his waiting suitcase, then back to her. "If I don't pack my stuff, can we stay?"

Now all the lollygagging made sense. He thought if he dragged his heels long enough, time would run out and they'd have to remain in Liberty Creek. Kid logic, she mused with a grin. You had to love it.

So, despite the fact that she'd found them a lovely new town house and had made all kinds of arrangements for them in Boston, she stood back from her usual practicality and reconsidered. Again. Only this time when she looked, the path was so obvious, she couldn't believe she'd missed seeing it before. Her mother's offer echoed in her mind, and Holly realized that for the first time in years, she had a viable option other than the circumstances she'd been forced to accept.

"Do you really want to live here?" she asked.

"Yes!" Swiveling around to his knees, he fixed her with a hopeful look. "Can we, Mom? Please?"

"Well, we have to get you registered at school, but I'm sure Mrs. Rogers can help us with that." The very capable young mother—now of four—might even have enough pull to get Chase into Cody's class, which would make the transition that much easier for him. But Holly didn't want to get his hopes up, so she kept that possibility to herself while making a mental note to call Sharon about it.

"I promise to help with the chores around

here," Chase went on excitedly, "and I can play junior football with Cody and his brothers."

"Or soccer," she suggested in an attempt to aim him toward a safer sport.

Her efforts earned her a smirk of disdain. "Soccer's boring. No one ever scores."

Since she had no ready comeback for that, she decided to table their sports conversation until later. "My phone's in my room. Why don't you go call Cody and tell him the good news while I talk to your grandmother?"

"Okay." He bounded into the hallway, and she heard him greet the lady in question with a chipper, "We're staying with you, Grams!"

From the surprised *oof* that followed, Holly guessed that he'd squeezed the stuffing out of their favorite diva before scurrying down the hall. Standing, she joined her mother on the upstairs landing with a smile. "I guess I don't have to tell you the news."

Genuine tears shined in the former actress's eyes as she grasped Holly's hands tightly. "I'm thrilled that you've decided to stay. I didn't know how I was going to bring myself to say goodbye, much less live here in this big, empty house without you and Chase."

"It would've been a lot quieter," Holly pointed out as they walked downstairs arm in arm.

"But that's the problem. This place is full of memories of the two of you now, and I would have missed you terribly."

"And we'd miss you, too," Holly assured her with a fond smile. Then, because now felt like the right time, she added a single word filled with meaning for both of them. "Mom."

The tears sprang up again, but this time they overflowed despite her efforts to blink them away. "Thank you, Holly. Hearing that from you is the most precious gift you could possibly give me."

Holly embraced her, sending up a silent thanks to God for helping her find a way to accept the truth and keep this quirky, loving woman in her life. Whatever mistakes she'd made in the past, Daphne Mills had always acted with her daughter's best interests first and foremost in her mind. Holly suspected that she had some more sorting out to do to enable her to more comfortably exist in her new family structure, but she was confident she could make it happen.

After all, she was her mother's daughter. And the Mills women never quit on the people they loved.

That thought reminded her that there was one more person she needed to share her good news with, and she gently pulled away. "Are you okay?"

Nodding, her mom gave her a knowing smile. "Go talk to Sam. I'll keep an eye on Chase until you get back."

Holly gave her another quick hug, then hurried out the front door and around the hedge that separated the two yards from one another. She found Sam under the hood of his work truck, and the muttering she heard alerted her that something in the engine was giving him a hard time. Not wanting to startle him, she stood on tiptoe and leaned over the radiator to look inside.

When their eyes met, he gave her a wry grin. "Sorry. Too loud?"

"No." He tilted his head dubiously, and she laughed. "Got a minute?"

"Sure."

And, as he'd done so many times since she first met him, he dropped what he was doing and gave her his full attention. When he pulled a rag from the back pocket of his jeans to wipe his hands, the very familiar action filled her with a rush of emotion for this kind, gentle man who'd fought his way out of his troubled past and had become her everyday hero.

Suddenly, she didn't know what to say. His

expectant look prompted her to shove her brain back into gear and explain why she'd interrupted him. "Chase and I have been talking, and I was just wondering something."

"What's that?"

Struggling to sound reasonably mature, she waited a beat before continuing. "How you'd feel if we changed our plans about going back to Boston."

Hope flared in his eyes, quickly doused by a wariness that she knew was born of more anguish than anyone should have to bear. "If you're asking my opinion, I think you should go wherever you and Chase will be the happiest."

Taking a step closer, she smiled up at him. "We both agree we'd be happiest right here."

"Here?" Sam echoed, as if he couldn't quite believe what he'd heard. "In Liberty Creek?"

When she nodded, he let out a whoop of joy and swept her into a hug, spinning her around as if she was a little girl. Setting her on her feet, he stole her breath with a long kiss filled with the same emotions she'd been feeling but hadn't had the nerve to confess to him.

Resting his forehead on hers, he let out a sigh so deep, she could almost feel the anxiety leaving his body. "I love you, Holly. I really didn't want you to go."

Framing his weathered face in her hands, she kissed him lightly and then smiled. "I love you, too, Sam. And so does Chase. More than you'll ever know."

Epilogue

"Happy Thanksgiving!"

At the sound of their Savannah visitors, Chase came bolting in from the living room, which was already full of Calhouns. Launching himself at their guests, he hugged them all fiercely, then stepped back and announced, "Mom burned the turkey."

Silence descended on the excited group, and they stared at Holly in disbelief. Rolling her eyes in the gesture Sam knew all too well, she laughed. "He's kidding. Everything's humming along, right on schedule. How was your flight?"

"Just fine," Don assured her as he and Sam shook hands. Holly made quick introductions, and Sam had to give the Frederickses credit for selling the idea that it was the first time they'd connected with him.

"Your sisters wish they could've come along," Gloria added, "but we'll see them when y'all come down for Christmas. They both send you and Chase their best." Another awkward silence, then she seemed to realize what she'd said and blushed in embarrassment. "Your cousins, I mean."

"Don't worry about it," Holly said, hugging her around the shoulders. "We'll get used to it eventually. We're family, and that's what really matters, right?"

"Right," Gloria agreed, clearly relieved to be let off the hook so easily.

Daphne appeared in the graceful archway, a joyful smile lighting her face. "It's wonderful to see you two. What do you think of my fixer-upper now?"

"It's beautiful," her sister said, giving her a long hug. "Just the way you always knew it could be."

"Sam and Holly worked wonders with this place," Daphne continued, beaming at her daughter and then him. "If it weren't for them, I'd still be wandering around the design store, hopelessly confused."

"I doubt that," Sam commented, grinning at his artistic consultant. "You Mills ladies have a knack for that kinda thing. I'm just the muscle."

"And me," Chase added eagerly, tugging his hand.

Sam chuckled and ruffled his hair. "And you. Speaking of helping, I could use some of it outside."

"Cool!"

As he dashed off to find the mini work jacket Sam had bought for him, Holly said, "While you're out there, could you bring in a couple of those squashes from the patio table? I'll be ready for them soon."

"Which ones?" he asked. "There's a whole pile of 'em."

Letting out an exasperated sigh, she shook her head in resignation. "Never mind. I'll get them myself."

"Meantime, come in and meet everyone," Daphne urged, linking arms with each of her visitors. "Sam's family is joining us for dinner, and there's a whole passel of them."

"She sounds more Southern all the time," Holly murmured as she and Sam followed Chase out to the patio.

"She sounds more like *you* all the time," Sam clarified, dropping an arm around her shoulders as they went down the brick steps he'd finished building in the nick of time.

"Yeah, I guess she does. Weird, huh?"

"Nice," he corrected her with a grin. "I always did like your accent."

"Did you?" she teased, draping her arms over his shoulders with a little smirk. "And what else did you like?"

Sam made a show of thinking that over, then grinned back. "Everything."

"Ooo, good answer," she approved, adding a quick kiss. "Just for that, you get a drumstick."

This was his opening, he thought, and he gathered up his courage for one of the most intimidating things he'd ever done. He'd been shot at, wounded, nearly destroyed by Nate's death, but what he was about to do came with a different kind of risk. He really hoped he'd never have to do it again.

"Chase, come here a minute, wouldya?" The boy loped over, and when they were all together, Sam took a moment to steady his nerves. Then, before he completely chickened out, he launched into the speech he'd spent days preparing.

"When I first met you two, I was a real mess. Everything was hard for me, and I didn't know how to make things better. But you did. You believed in me," he went on, smiling at Holly, "and you made me feel like a hero."

This smile was for Chase, who stared up at him with the trusting look he treasured from the boy who'd lost his own father so young.

"You are a hero, Sam," the boy assured him eagerly. "Me and the guys on the football team think you're the best."

"I really appreciate that, bud." Reaching into the front pocket of his one good pair of trousers, he pulled out a velvet box and closed it in his hand before kneeling in front of Holly. When he met her eyes, they were brilliantly blue and shining with emotion, and it struck him that those strong, unwavering feelings were for him. For a guy who'd convinced himself he'd never be able to have that in his life, it was a humbling feeling.

"I've got work to do still, but I won't stop until I'm the kind of man you both deserve." Opening the box with a little creak, he lifted his gaze to hers and took the most terrifying leap of his life. "In the meantime, will you marry me?"

Chase let out a delighted whoop, barreling into them for an exuberant hug that made it clear what his answer was. Holly was more reserved, but the joy lighting her features was all the answer Sam needed.

"Yes, I will," she said in a voice that didn't

hesitate even the slightest bit, nodding for good measure.

Reaching out, she pulled her son in close while Sam slid the antique setting onto her finger. Holding her hand out to admire the sparkling ring, she kissed the top of Chase's head and then brought Sam's lips to hers. Drawing back, she bathed him in the beautiful smile he was looking forward to seeing every day for the rest of his life.

"This is awesome," Chase announced, fist-bumping Sam in approval. "We're gonna make a great family."

"Y'know what?" Sam said, returning his fiancée's smile with a confident one of his own. "I think you're right."

* * * * *

Dear Reader,

Thanks so much for following me to Liberty Creek!

Months ago, I stumbled across a picture of a quaint New England town, and the wheels in my head started spinning. My reaction to the back-in-time feeling became Holly's, and her story began to take shape. Spunky as she was, she had a lot more to contend with than she realized, which is something many of us can relate to. Often, just when we think we've got a handle on what's going on around us, things change, and we have to adjust to the new reality we face. It isn't easy, but Holly's determination and unshakable faith—along with her love for her son—kept her going.

When Sam Calhoun appeared in that very first scene, I didn't know his whole story yet, but I knew it was worth telling. Part of him was stranded in the past, no matter how hard he tried to reclaim control of his life. Once he found a way to forgive himself—and God—for Nate's death, he was finally able to embrace a future with the family he'd given up hoping for. So many military veterans carry burdens like his, experiences that make it difficult for them to resume the lives they enjoyed before their service. The courage they display every day is inspiring. With this story, I hope I've honored the sacrifices they and their families have made to keep our country safer.

This is the first of four books set in Liberty Creek, and I'm thrilled to be working on another series for Love Inspired. If you'd like to stop in and see what I've been up to, you'll find me online at www.miaross.com, Facebook, Twitter and Goodreads. While you're there, send me a message in your favorite format. I'd love to hear from you!

Mia Ross

Get 2 Free Books,

Plus 2 Free Gifts—

just for trying the Reader Service!

LIS17R2

Get 2 Free Books,
Plus 2 Free Gifts—
just for trying the Reader Service!

HOMETOWN HEARTS ♥

YES! Please send me **The Hometown Hearts Collection** in Larger Print. This collection begins with 3 FREE books and 2 FREE gifts in the first shipment. Along with my 3 free books, I'll also get the next 4 books from the Hometown Hearts Collection, in LARGER PRINT, which I may either return and owe nothing, or keep for the low price of $4.99 U.S./ $5.89 CDN each plus $2.99 for shipping and handling per shipment*. If I decide to continue, about once a month for 8 months I will get 6 or 7 more books, but will only need to pay for 4. That means 2 or 3 books in every shipment will be FREE! If I decide to keep the entire collection, I'll have paid for only 32 books because 19 books are FREE! I understand that accepting the 3 free books and gifts places me under no obligation to buy anything. I can always return a shipment and cancel at any time. My free books and gifts are mine to keep no matter what I decide.

262 HCN 3432 462 HCN 3432

Name	(PLEASE PRINT)	
Address		Apt. #
City	State/Prov.	Zip/Postal Code

Signature (if under 18, a parent or guardian must sign)

Mail to the **Reader Service:**

IN U.S.A.: P.O. Box 1867, Buffalo, NY. 14240-1867
IN CANADA: P.O. Box 609, Fort Erie, Ontario L2A 5X3

* Terms and prices subject to change without notice. Prices do not include applicable taxes. Sales tax applicable in NY. Canadian residents will be charged applicable taxes. This offer is limited to one order per household. All orders subject to approval. Credit or debit balances in a customer's account(s) may be offset by any other outstanding balance owed by or to the customer. Please allow 4 to 6 weeks for delivery. Offer available while quantities last. Offer not available to Quebec residents.

Your Privacy—The Reader Service is committed to protecting your privacy. Our Privacy Policy is available online at www.ReaderService.com or upon request from the Reader Service.

We make a portion of our mailing list available to reputable third parties that offer products we believe may interest you. If you prefer that we not exchange your name with third parties, or if you wish to clarify or modify your communication preferences, please visit us at www.ReaderService.com/consumerschoice or write to us at Reader Service Preference Service, P.O. Box 9062, Buffalo, NY. 14240-9062. Include your complete name and address.

READERSERVICE.COM

Manage your account online!

- Review your order history
- Manage your payments
- Update your address

We've designed the Reader Service website just for you.

Enjoy all the features!

- Discover new series available to you, and read excerpts from any series.
- Respond to mailings and special monthly offers.
- Browse the Bonus Bucks catalog and online-only exculsives.
- Share your feedback.

Visit us at:

ReaderService.com

RS16R